C000053301

TWO WEEKS TO LIVE

TWO WEEKS
TO LIVE

PETER ASPINALL

Copyright © 2019 Peter Aspinall

The moral right of the author has been asserted.

Apart from any fair dealing for the purposes of research or private study,
or criticism or review, as permitted under the Copyright, Designs and Patents
Act 1988, this publication may only be reproduced, stored or transmitted, in
any form or by any means, with the prior permission in writing of the
publishers, or in the case of reprographic reproduction in accordance with
the terms of licences issued by the Copyright Licensing Agency. Enquiries
concerning reproduction outside those terms should be sent to the publishers.

This is a work of fiction. Names, characters, businesses, places, events
and incidents are either the products of the author's imagination
or used in a fictitious manner. Any resemblance to actual persons,
living or dead, or actual events is purely coincidental.

Matador
9 Priory Business Park,
Wistow Road, Kibworth Beauchamp,
Leicestershire. LE8 0RX
Tel: 0116 279 2299
Email: books@troubador.co.uk
Web: www.troubador.co.uk/matador
Twitter: @matadorbooks

ISBN 978 1789018 523

British Library Cataloguing in Publication Data.
A catalogue record for this book is available from the British Library.

Printed and bound in the UK by TJ International, Padstow, Cornwall
Typeset in 11pt Adobe Garamond Pro by Troubador Publishing Ltd, Leicester, UK

Matador is an imprint of Troubador Publishing Ltd

To Gillian, my beloved muse and mentor.

FOREWORD

A steroids are roughly-hewn boulders cascading through space, the vast majority of them orbiting in an unruly fashion between Mars and Jupiter. They are mostly made up of primordial metal, rock, ice and dust.

Despite hurtling through an almost unimaginably immense area of mainly nothing, these nomadic, celestial beasts have this irksome habit of tilting off course and crashing into planets and moons on a random, but reasonably regular basis.

They have been doing this for many, many millions of years. Asteroids range from the size of a small car to the considerably alarming bulk of 900 kilometres across, collision damage inflicted pro rata.

Until 1994, humans had never witnessed a cosmic impact. Then, thanks to the ingenuity of a particularly useful bit of space kit called the Hubble Space Telescope, scientists were able to watch a comet (an asteroid's cousin named Shoemaker-Levy 9) go head to head with Jupiter. Lukewarm sceptics warned of a damp squib, more of a fizzle than a frenzy, countering that the comet was a 'string of fragments' rather than an intimidating chunky monolith taking its chances with by far the biggest planet in our solar system. Come and have a go if you think you're hard enough taunted Jupiter.

The impacts began in July 1994 and one 'fragment' called Nucleus G – approximately the size of Scafell Pike – struck the massive planet with the explosive force of about six million megatonnes, or 75 times the power of all the nuclear weapons in known existence. Erstwhile sceptics gasped, produced a few red-faced excuses and immediately started to dig bunkers in their back gardens while telescopes all over planet Earth reached skywards to search the heavens for the threat of an incoming Armageddon.

Part One

ONE

George Longworth had been to see the specialist. It
was his fourth visit. The cancer in his stomach was
as real and intimidating as it had always been, but as
far as the medics could establish, was contained. It had not
spread. Not yet. George had to live with it…as best as he
could and for as long as he could. Lifestyle and diet had to
improve. Medication had to be taken. Doctor's orders.

George's illness meant he could no longer work as a car
mechanic and since the enforced laying up of the spanner
and plug socket three months earlier, he had attempted to
maintain a daily routine. George, 52, liked routine. It gave
his life shape and meaning. If he was being honest, it made
him feel like he still had a job, the one he missed so much.
So, he reluctantly hauled his considerable frame out of bed
at 7.00am each morning, continued to shave and wash
in relative silence next to an unflushed toilet (so as not to

awaken she who must yet be asleep) and still ate breakfast alone downstairs in the chilly kitchen/diner, standing next to and leaning on the fridge just as he had always done. One concession to change still made him tut with exasperation every time he pulled open the kitchen cupboard. What the bloody hell was luxury muesli anyway? What was wrong with white toast? Does that cancer specialist know everything?

Ten minutes later Gaynor Longworth joined her husband in the kitchen/diner, wished him a cheery good morning, kissed him on the cheek and rinsed his luxury muesli bowl under the cold tap. She kept the water running to submerge an egg she had placed in a small saucepan. 'Put one in there for me…no make that two,' came the cry as Larry tumbled down the stairs and into the kitchen/diner, hair dishevelled, school blazer dishevelled, everything dishevelled in fact.

Larry Longworth was the 16-year-old son of George and Gaynor and was in his last year of comprehensive education. He wasn't a particularly studious pupil and didn't know what the future held after he had finished his GCSEs that summer. He did know that he didn't want to be a car mechanic like his dad. He couldn't tell a camshaft from a pit shaft. Larry cast a disparaging glance at the half-open box of luxury muesli and watched his mother's well-balanced teaspoon gently immerse the first of his two eggs into the warming water.

'Better stick one in for our Katie as well. She's tried Dad's new muesli and said it was like eating the wood shavings off a rabbit hutch floor with the droppings still in it.'

'She has quite a way with words has that young girl,' remarked George, filling the kettle. 'That's exactly what it tastes like.'

4

Larry smiled. Dad still had his sense of humour despite the enemy within. He pulled his smart phone out of his pocket and stroked the screen lovingly.

'You spend far too much time gazing at that bloody thing,' snapped his father. 'The entire teenage population in this town walks around with a phone sticking out in front of them like some kind of extra limb. They're like the living dead, half-comatose zombies bumping into grannies and tripping over kerbs.'

Larry flicked his phone. 'My mate in America – who I talk to on this bloody thing – tells me his dad is an amateur astronomer and that he's just spotted a rogue asteroid hurtling through space millions of miles away. He reckons it may come close to Earth, might even crash straight into it, killing us all.'

He stopped, appeared puzzled and added, 'What is an asteroid anyway?'

TWO

'Come on Bernard. Let's go.'

Bernard the St Bernard dog was George's trusted friend and soul mate. Apart from the occasional twitch of the tail, this Merlin of the canine world was unflappable. He offered his human companion camaraderie, sage counsel and a patient, compassionate ear. Bernard, unlike George, wholly appreciated early retirement. Walks had proliferated, become longer and welcomingly routine. On-lead time was greatly increased, and Bernard had quickly learned that mid-morning was the start time for walk number one. Once George was alone.

It was mid-morning now and an expectant hound had been holding the leash in his mouth for at least ten minutes. Saliva dripped and formed a small pool on the murky coir mat behind the front door.

Master and dog set off down the road, past a row of cars illegally half-parked on the pavement as twin streams of seemingly endless traffic filled the rest of the highway.

'There was nothing like this amount of traffic on the roads when I first started driving', George informed Bernard with a deep sigh. 'Look at that bloody lot. Going nowhere, not very fast.'

Along uneven flags and past verge-side hedges they strolled. A wren chirred. George searched his mind for another subject to talk about with a most convivial conversational partner. Bernard was a good listener and rarely disagreed, even with George's more forthright opinions.

'Have you noticed the subtle hints being dropped about going abroad on holiday?' asked George.

'Have they mentioned it to you yet Bernard? There's a new bottle of suntan lotion next to my shaving mirror in the bathroom and Gaynor keeps telling me how cheap flights are, these days. I feel the slow creep of a family conspiracy. The drip, drip, drip of propaganda. Have you sensed it Bernard? I suspect you have.'

George often talked to his dog. Gaynor complained that Bernard received more attention than she did. George replied that she was talking nonsense and told her to fetch his slippers. Gaynor had smiled outwardly and inwardly. She was only too aware of the mighty burden of stomach cancer weighing heavily on her husband's slightly sagging shoulders and was happy when she came across evidence of his knavish, waspish sense of humour still intact.

George and Bernard turned off the car park masquerading as a main carriageway on to a less beaten track, a footpath that led to a small wood alongside a grassy hill that had started life as a spoil heap. A bullfinch settled contentedly in a beech tree and looked plump. Voles cowered.

George let Bernard off the lead, but the faithful hound continued to plod contentedly alongside his master. He was still in the mood for a chat and George duly obliged. 'I'll tell you what Bernard...I could bloody well murder a fag. Another avenue of pleasure closed down by the specialist. Cure cancer by taking all enjoyment out of life. That's his motto. He asked me if I'd stopped drinking and I told him I was just having a few sherbets at home at the weekend. He even tutted and shook his head at that. I'm not sure if he's a hospital consultant or a chief inspector in the fun police. Enjoying yourself son? We'll soon put a stop to that. Ten years' hard labour is what's coming your way my lad.'

George stopped, bent down and gently pulled Bernard's lugubrious face into his, rubbing the dog's ears as he did so.

'I wish I had ten years hard labour left in me Bernard,' he said wistfully. 'I'll tell you that for free and bloody gratis. Come on, let's make our way back home. Scenic route?'

THREE

George was sitting on the sofa flicking through the channels on the television by roughly prodding the remote control with a time-worn index finger that was slightly too large for the job.

'I can't believe how many channels there are on this thing,' he groused. But then he smiled. He had come across an oft repeated episode of "Rising Damp" on ITV 28.

'This will cheer us both up Katie,' he announced to his daughter who was perched alongside him. 'That Leonard Rossiter, now he's what I call a classic comedian.'

It was 5.30 pm on a Monday afternoon. Drizzle descended from a slate sky. It was 19-year-old Katie's day off and trainee hairdressers didn't work Mondays. Katie had tried college after leaving school with a smattering of half-decent GCSEs. She had intended to become a teacher like her mum but had decided that this particular choice of career involved far too much stress, mainly because her own mother moaned about it so much. Salary not enough – especially now she was the family's principal wage-earner – and petulant pupils behaving badly. Hairdressing, Katie reasoned, didn't come home with you.

'Do you think I need cheering up Dad?' she asked as Rigsby yet again tried to impress Miss Jones by showing her the new sports car he had just bought.

'Just a figure of speech,' replied George. 'That Richard Beckinsale's a right good-looking lad, isn't he?'

'Do you know what would cheer me up Dad? A holiday. A foreign holiday in the sun. Mum would like it and wouldn't you after…after all you've been through…at the hospital and all the rest of it?' Katie tailed off, squirming on her seat and slightly embarrassed as she struggled to find the appropriate words to guide her through the treacherous waters surrounding her dad's illness.

'Aye, well, erm,' replied George, making a mental note of the propaganda up-grade before plonking himself firmly on the fence. 'We'll have to wait and see.'

'Ibiza, now that would be lovely,' murmured Kate.

'Yeh, but it's full of blokes who have turned into women after too many late nights,' scoffed George. 'It's fifty quid just to get into a nightclub and then it's about fifteen quid a pint. That's what that young apprentice at the garage told me anyway. Fifteen quid a pint! No wonder they all take drugs.'

'I daresay Ibiza does have its seedier parts,' sniffed Katie, 'but that's surely true of anywhere in the world and there are parts of the island that are very beautiful and tranquil. That's what the young girl who washes the customers' hair told me anyway.'

'And would our Bernard like it?' asked George. The dog, slumbering gently aboard his master's feet, lifted an ear as he acknowledged his name being mentioned.

'He'd have to go into kennels,' replied Katie.

'Oh, you wouldn't like that at all would you Bernie boy', replied George, nudging Bernard in the ribs with a besocked big toe. The dog shook his head as if in agreement and Katie laughed.

'What's amusing you?' asked Gaynor, walking into the lounge with a cup of tea and settling down next to her daughter on the sofa.

'Bernard's just told us that he doesn't mind at all if we all go on holiday together to Ibiza without him', chuckled Katie. 'He's really looking forward to meeting some new mates in the kennels.'

'That's most considerate of him,' replied Gaynor. 'That means there are no obstacles in the way', casting her husband a furtive glance.

George scowled and tutted as he took on board the family conspiracy unfolding around him. Gaynor had been dropping hints of an impromptu overseas holiday for several days and experience had taught him that whenever his wife scattered seeds in the ground, copious amounts of flourishing foliage usually followed. A long history of being Captain Grumpy meant that he felt obliged to whine and moan about expensive trips abroad, but now the enemy within was about to change all that. Deep inside George knew how much the holiday meant, not only to his nearest and dearest, but also to himself.

None of them knew what tomorrow would bring.

FOUR

Harry Pickford was hardening off his sweet peas in his home-made raised bed next to the fence when he lifted his head and sneaked a peek into the garden next door. He looked for George but could only see Bernard who was flat out on the patio gnawing the end of a most unappetising-looking bone.

'Now then Bernard, where's that Georgie boy gone?' shouted Harry before turning his head slightly as if there was a chance of a reply coming his way. The dog cast him a rheumy eye and carried on gnawing.

'You'll be coming to the hospital with me if you carry on asking that dog daft questions', barked George, bustling his way along the side of the house, pushing his way past far too many re-cycling bins half-blocking the narrow gap before making his way into the garden. 'The psychiatric department is just next door.'

'Gaynor tells me you talk to the dog more than you do to her, so I'll book you in on the couch next to me', replied Harry, chuckling to himself. George replied, 'She told me that I never listen to a word she says. That's what I think she said anyway.'

Harry chortled and carried on the banter. 'Bernard's just told me you're all going on holiday and leaving him behind. He isn't too happy. He's just had a word with me about it.'

George and Harry had been neighbours and good friends for more than 20 years. Harry and his wife Esme had helped to wet the heads of both their neighbours' children, had proved to be dependable baby-sitters as they got older and today were valued spare key holders to both front and back doors as the teenage years delivered the time-served combination of amnesia and carelessness.

The two families harboured few secrets from each another, plans for an imminent foreign holiday patently not one of them.

'That Gaynor's been jangling it again then', remarked George with a wry grin. 'It's all propaganda and pressure by the family because of you-know-what. I haven't confirmed.'

Harry cast him a knowing look. Good neighbourliness extended all the way to sharing medical bulletins from the hospital and Harry was only too aware of the angst eating away at the beating heart of what outwardly appeared to be a family fretting over only customary concerns such as under-age alcohol intake and unsuitable boyfriends with cor' blimey haircuts.

'Do you want to come around and take a look at these bedding plants in the greenhouse?' shouted George over the fence, deliberately changing the subject. 'I think they've got some terrible disease.'

Harry made his way around the side of his neighbour's house, irritably kicked the blue re-cycling bin (clean bottles and plastic, no cardboard) and together the two men walked into the glasshouse.

George ran a loving hand over the young tomato plants emerging proudly out of damp grow-bags on raised side benches and held his fingers to his nose. 'I love the smell of the leaves. Somebody should bottle that and sell it in some fancy London department store. About fifty pounds a pop. What man could resist the delicate perfume of a vine-ripened piccolo tomato?' he remarked to no-one in particular. He led Harry to his workbench at the bottom of the greenhouse and pulled a potted primula into handling range.

'Just try lifting it gently by the stem.'

Harry plucked delicately at the young plant and it came away in his hand, the roots severed just below the surface of the soil.

'That can't be right can it Percy Thrower?' sniffed George.

'Vine weevil,' diagnosed Harry. 'Otherwise known in the horticultural trade as complete and utter bastards. The grubs get in the soil and chew through the roots of the plant. You'll need to treat all your containers and kill off the little blighters, so they don't spread.'

'A bit like stomach cancer then,' said George softly. 'You sound like the consultant at the hospital.'

'Sorry,' replied Harry in a low voice. 'I didn't mean to, er, well, I didn't mean anything really.'

'No, no, it's me who should be apologising,' replied George, blushing slightly. 'It's just that when I'm reminded of what's happening to me, I let it get to me and know that I shouldn't.'

George shook his head and took the primula out of Harry's hand. 'Come on, let's go and see if we can persuade Bernard to let me go on this holiday.'

FIVE

Larry Longworth was sitting at the back of the science class paying a bit of attention, which made a change. The young teacher, a newly-qualified Mr Gibbons, was talking about the solar system and the movement of the earth around the sun. This full orbit, he explained, took 365 days, a journey time which created our year. He told the class that the earth travelled around the sun at a speed of about 67,000 miles an hour and that the tilt of the earth, its varying distances from the sun combined with the influence of the moon helped to create the four seasons.

He asked if there were any questions and failed to disguise a scintilla of surprise when, from the far reaches of the classroom, young Longworth's arm reached for the heavens. He surely wanted to use the toilet.

'Sir, what's an asteroid?' were the most unexpected words tumbling from the teenager's lips.

The teacher realised he was diverting off course somewhat, but at least the question was space-related, while he also felt the need to retain the pupil's interest as it was, after all, the first time he'd shown any.

'An asteroid is a large rock which hurtles through space. They're sometimes called comets. There are millions of them out there. It is believed they could be left over from the big bang which, as some of you may already know, created the universe about four billion years ago.'

The half-stifled giggles filling the room told Mr Gibbons that the his choice of the phase 'big bang' was not a wise one in front of a mixed classroom full of 16-year-olds and the plot was about to get even thicker when on the front row, Jenny Seagrove raised her hand and, with a puzzled frown, announced, 'Sir, I thought it was God who created the universe.'

A trilling bell in the corridor outside marked the end of the class, a bell that truly save the rookie teacher. Well, almost. For as the pupils filed past him on their way out, Larry Longworth sidled up alongside the teacher's desk and asked him another question. Two questions in two minutes, prior to which there had been none in almost two terms. This boy was surely destined to become a bus driver.

'Wasn't it an asteroid crashing into earth that wiped out the dinosaurs about sixty-five years ago sir?'

'Er, about sixty-five million years ago Larry,' replied the teacher, placing the emphasis on the million. 'Not when Bill Haley was in the charts, although he did have a few comets. But yes, you're right, or that's the popular theory anyway. They've quite recently discovered the enormous crater it left behind. Somewhere just off the Mexican coast if my memory serves me correctly. Larry…may I ask how you know that and what's with the sudden interest in asteroids?'

'I asked Professor Google about the dinosaur thing. It's because I link up with this American guy called Michael Berlingo on a social media site and he tells me that his dad is an amateur astronomer. He's installed a top of the range telescope in his house and he watches for asteroids travelling through space. He reckons he's spotted one that's heading towards Earth, but apparently, he's said the same thing before and we're all still waiting for the explosion. So, what would happen if another asteroid did come crashing into the earth. Would we all be wiped out like the dinosaurs?'

'If it's a big one, then more than likely,' replied Mr Gibbons, stacking exercise books and glancing anxiously at the clock on the wall. 'But don't let this distract you from the homework that's due in next Wednesday young Larry my lad. And let's have it in on time for a change. Annihilation by asteroid will not qualify as an acceptable excuse for tardiness.'

Mr Gibbons picked up his paperwork and marched out of the room with the hint of a smug smile resting on his lips.

SIX

'Bernard informs me that he'd rather stay with Harry next door rather than go into kennels. He says he's not bothered about meeting new mates because you can't teach an old dog new tricks.'

George turned and smiled at his wife situated on the far end of the couch. Coronation Street had just finished, and George thought it a rather opportune moment to speak. Anything but watch the adverts.

'So, that means we are going on holiday then does it?' replied Gaynor, in a tone which indicated she remained to be convinced.

'I think we both know that was always going to be the ultimate outcome,' mumbled George.

'Where shall we go then?' demanded Gaynor, leaping head first through the half-open window of opportunity. 'It must be ten years since we went abroad. You had a good

19

excuse when the kids were young, but let's face it, you never were keen on those 'bloody foreigners' as you used to call them and when we actually made it to Spain you were continually bleating about what havoc the food was wreaking on your digestive system. Let's have it right George, if there was a hint of garlic on the menu, you were heading for the nearest toilet.'

George smirked then nodded in tacit agreement before digging deep into previously untapped reserves of character and determination. 'I was thinking of going to Australia actually.'

'Australia!' gasped Gaynor. 'How much will that cost?'

'There you go. The hint of spending a few bob on the menu and you head straight for the nearest toilet.'

'Okay, point made,' replied Gaynor. 'But I'm the only person bringing in any meaningful money into this house – at the moment,' she added, rather uncertainly.

'Perhaps, under the circumstances, money doesn't really matter anymore,' replied George quietly.

Gaynor paused and looked at her husband with a mix of surprise and admiration. 'You're so right love', leaning across two cushions and kissing him affectionately on the cheek.

'I'll go and tell the kids. Have you got a surf board?'

▼

'It was your Dad's idea, not mine,' explained Gaynor.

Mum was breaking the big holiday news to Katie and Larry in the kitchen/diner as the children prepared tea for all the family. She frowned as Larry poured a random quantity of uncooked rice into a frying pan and turned up the heat. The kids making tea had been George's idea as well.

'But Australia!' gasped Katie. 'Last summer he was moaning because it was too far to drive to Bournemouth, now he's packing his Speedos for Bondi beach. What's got into him?'

A slightly uneasy silence descended because they all knew the answer. But it was a rhetorical question anyway and as Gaynor the English teacher might have pointed out, rhetorical questions don't require answers.

'We'll have to go at Easter. I know it's only a few weeks off, but I don't want to wait until summer,' said Gaynor. 'Which means two weeks away which will take up all the school holidays, but you need at least a fortnight when you're travelling as far as Australia. It's the other side of the world you know.'

'Really Mum? And there's me thinking it was the other side of the West Midlands,' smirked Katie.

'A little bit of sarcasm goes a long way thank you, young lady,' snapped Gaynor, before turning her attention to her son. 'Larry, are you going to add some liquid to that rice you're incinerating in the pan?'

'I'm making fried rice Mum. It was going to be a bloody surprise.'

'It certainly will be a bloody surprise if you don't boil it first. I knew they should never have scrapped domestic science.'

Katie intervened. 'I'll sort it Mum. Go and sit down with Dad and check that he's not made a mistake or changed his mind about this holiday. Get him to concentrate on Rigsby's new sports car.'

Gaynor cast her daughter a perplexed look but decided to leave it. She walked back into the lounge and settled

21

down next to her husband on the sofa. 'Gordon Ramsay's making the tea, but I suspect the only similarity with one of his gourmet dishes will be the side helping of bad language. Brace yourself for a large helping of disappointment.

By the way, is Rigsby's new sports car an MG?'

SEVEN

'Young Charlotte here would like some subtle blonde highlights. Are you alright with that Katie?'

So spoke Carol, the manager of the hairdressing salon, handing Katie more responsibility than she had ever handled before. Washing, trimming and blow-drying had occupied her working hours so far. Blonde highlights were a whole new ball game.

'I'll help you Katie,' said Carol, ushering young Charlotte over to her chair in front of the mirror. 'Are you both okay with that?'

Twin nods indicated relatively calm waters ahead, Carol heading off to make the coffees and so hand Katie the public relations aspect of the job. The teenager fell straight back on old faithful as she ran her fingers through the customer's hair.

'Are you going on holiday this summer Charlotte?'

'Yep, Majorca, two weeks in the sun with my boyfriend. It's the first time we've been on holiday together.'

'Well, you know what they say don't you?' replied Katie.

'No, what?'

'If you can both survive a fortnight together in a foreign country without a serious fall-out, then you might as well get married.'

'I've never heard that before. Is it true?'

'Dunno,' shrugged Katie. 'I think I read it in one of those posh women's magazines which means it probably must be. '

Charlotte looked slightly bemused, but also shrugged and continued the conversation.' We were originally going to do Australia, but it all got a bit complicated, you know all the visa stuff and all the forms to fill in.'

Katie's hands came to a standstill. 'What, you need a visa to go on holiday in Australia?' she asked, rather abruptly and failing to disguise the concern in her voice.

'Apparently,' replied young Charlotte. 'Shane – that's my boyfriend – that's what he reckoned anyway. He said that he couldn't be bothered with all the fuss. That's why we're going to Majorca instead.'

Carol returned with three cups of coffee on a tray. Katie turned to her boss and blurted, 'Is it true you need a visa to go to Australia?'

'I think so,' said Carol, placing the tray on the spare chair next door. 'That's a rather strange question to ask. 'Are you going there Katie?'

'Think so. That's the plan at least. Can I have all Easter off by the way?'

▼

'We all need visas to go to Australia,' was Katie's opening gambit as she rather breathlessly barged her way through the back door after work to find her mum busy preparing the evening meal in the kitchen/diner.

'It took me ten minutes to clean that frying pan after your gormless brother's outrageous attempt at fried rice,' came the reply. 'That's it, he's banned from the kitchen... but that's probably exactly the outcome he was looking for,' she added, talking to herself rather than her daughter. 'Perhaps he's not as gormless as I thought.'

'Mum, did you hear what I just said?'

'Yes, I know all about the visa thing. It's no big deal just for a holiday. You can apply on the internet, we'll just have to be quick. I've not told your Dad yet. The less to fret about, the better it will be. That's my theory anyway.'

'What's for tea?' asked Katie.

'Vegemite sandwiches and four tubes of Fosters. Is that fair dinkum?' sniggered Gaynor.

Katie smiled and sauntered into the lounge where her father was half-asleep on the sofa and listing badly to starboard. He straightened with a start and cursed noisily at the remote control.

'I'm really looking forward to Australia. Are you Dad?' said Katie, snuggling up next to her father.

'I most surely am my little pikelet,' grunted George, placing his arm around his daughter's shoulder and cuddling her into him. 'It will be all the family all together, a long way from home, but very close to each other when we actually get there.'

Katie placed her arms on her dad's shoulders and her head on his chest. She ran the fingers of one hand through the thick, gritty hair on the back of his head and dad held her close and for more seconds than it took for a quick affectionate hug. Katie felt tears welling but remembered what they had all agreed. We have to stay positive.

She lifted her head resolutely and looked her dad in the eye. 'Mum said she's making an Australian tea. Anything you fancy?'

George paused and replied, 'You can tell that bonza Shelagh of mine that I'll have a crocodile sandwich and make it snappy.'

Katie tumbled on to the carpet laughing.

EIGHT

The clear night sky over the state of Texas, USA was as black as ebony all the way to the distant heavens, a deep and bewildering canvas embedded with countless stars.

Maurice Berlingo pushed back a section of the roof on his house that opened rather ingeniously on specially fitted rollers and peered through the void. 'Perfect' he muttered to himself before slightly adjusting his telescope. From the attic he shouted down the stairs, 'Michael, come and take a look. The conditions are almost ideal.'

His teenage son leapt the narrow stairs two at a time and joined his father in his home-made observatory.

'I'm going to check out the simple star I found last night. I took a picture of it and if it's moved then there's every chance it will be an asteroid, probably a big one.'

Maurice switched on the computer connected to the telescope and filled half the screen with the shot of the darkened sky taken the night before. He refreshed the computer's memory which in turn re-aligned the telescope and after a few more instructions from the keyboard, a picture of the same area of space was produced and filled the other half of the screen.

Maurice peered at it intently and pointed an accusing finger.

'It's moved!' he exclaimed excitedly. 'It might not look much on the screen, but the reality is that's one hell of a beast of an asteroid and it's travelling mighty quick.'

'Where's it headed?' asked Michael.

'Hard to say. Asteroids are rocky objects in space, most of them orbiting the sun. They range enormously in size and are usually found between Mars and Jupiter, though some have more eccentric orbits. But if they are in orbit, they don't really head anywhere other than where they started out. But for reasons a rookie amateur like me doesn't quite understand, some do break their orbits and can eventually pass close to earth. And if a big one did just that and actually crashed into our planet, well, I reckon we can all kiss our sorry asses goodbye.'

'Didn't an asteroid see off the dinosaurs many millions of years ago?' asked Michael.

'Yep, sure did. It's not just the force of the explosive impact, it's the aftermath that makes the planet almost uninhabitable for many years. Wild, raging fires, earthquakes, tsunamis and vast quantities of dust and debris were blasted into the atmosphere. This blocks out the sun for season after season so that nothing grows, and everything dies. Well, virtually everything anyway.'

'Didn't you tell me a few weeks ago that another of the asteroids you'd discovered was going to crash into Earth?

I told an English guy called Larry all about it on Skype. Neither of us has heard any explosions yet.'

'Er, yes,' replied his dad, rather sheepishly. 'Got that one a bit wrong. Sorry.'

'So, is this new asteroid that you've just discovered heading our way?'

'Possibly. I'm just an amateur dabbling in what is a complicated science. Perhaps I'd be better keeping my theories to myself. Or perhaps I should call NASA again.'

'You might make a name for yourself one day Dad. You never know.'

NINE

A dejected George Longworth looked up at the clock ticking wearily on the wall of the GP's waiting room and sighed deeply.

As a regular patient with a grade one listed disease he surely deserved to be seen on time. This was not a slight cold or a dislocated sleeve, this was a real ailment, one demanding urgent medical attention, yet he had already been waiting half an hour. A nurse poked her head around a door, read his name off a list and used hand signals to indicate that George should follow her into the consultancy room.

Dr Tim Parkinson looked up from the computer screen on his desk, took off his glasses and leaned back in his chair.

'Hello George, sorry about the delay, how's life?'

'Boring,' replied George. 'No, I'll re-phrase that. Bloody boring. No job, no fun, no alcohol, nothing to look forward to.'

'Am I to assume that the hospital consultant has read the riot act to you?' posited his GP.

'The bloody matron? She sure has. She's even warned me that I can't even have a drink at the weekend now. I told her that I only share a bottle of cheap fizzy wine with Gaynor and blow the froth off a few bottled lagers in front of the television and she started to tut and shake her head like she was dealing with some kind of serial killer. Talking of which, have you ever tried luxury muesli?'

'Pardon?' asked the doctor.

'Nothing, it doesn't matter' replied George, grinning inanely.

'So, what can I do for you George?'

'Nothing medical actually, not unless the boffins have come up with a miracle cure for cancer since we last met. I want to ask your advice if you don't mind…seek your approval if the truth be known.'

'Run it up my flagpole,' replied the medic.

'Well, I'm thinking of going to Australia for a big blow-out holiday with all the family, all except Bernard of course. He's putting on a brave face, but deep down I know that he's really upset because we're planning on going to Sydney, Brisbane, the Great Barrier Reef, scuba diving, the whole nine yards. We can't afford it really, but in the light of recent developments on the medical front…what the hell.'

'Well, you'll still need to look after yourself and be aware of your condition.'

The doctor clicked and moved his mouse several times as he studied his shifting computer screen.

He added, 'I see you're on chemotherapy, so I assume the consultant has prescribed the tablets for you. I hope you're keeping up with your medication and I presume you will be taking them with you to Australia.'

'That's the plan. I get the tablets in cycles, each course lasting about three weeks. I've worked out that I'll be starting a new cycle just before I leave, so that should be alright then.'

'What's the Matron, sorry, the consultant I mean, said about the big adventure?'

'Er, not told her yet. If I tell her at all. I have this awful feeling that she's going to try and pull the plug on the entire thing. I don't think I could live with the disappointment. I know the family couldn't.'

Dr Parkinson pushed his chair and himself away from his desk and his computer and turned to face his patient. His face looked rather stern.

'You and I have known each other for many years George and ultimately the decision is yours. However, my advice to you is to inform the consultant of your plans. If you choose not to, and I suspect you're not going to, then I don't want to know. That would place me in an embarrassing position, so the only advice I'm officially handing out today is that you tell the consultant about your holiday. Do we understand each other?'

George nodded, stood up and shook the doctor's hand.

'I understand completely. It's all about that hypocrite's oath, the medical requirement to uphold ethical standards and all that caper, isn't it?'

'Something like that George', replied the doctor, smiling gently.

'I suppose, deep down, you don't really think that going to Australia is a good idea at all do you?' said George.

'On the contrary. All things considered, I think it's a wonderful idea', replied the GP. 'A real tonic for you and all the family after what you've all been through and it may even have some medical value.'

'Really, how do you work that one out?'

'Well, it's something to look forward to. Good for the soul and mental well-being possibly and looking forward to something was mentioned on the list of things that you miss.'

'Yeh, never thought about it that way. Let's hope you're right.'

George paused and thought for a few seconds. 'And as for the boozing at the weekend…does gleeful anticipation mean that the same medical value applies there too? What's your professional opinion on that one Doc?' he added, fully aware that he was pushing his luck a tad.

Dr Parkinson straightened his chair, re-fitted his glasses on to the top of his nose and peered over them at his patient.

'Well, not too sure about recommending alcohol to anyone under any circumstances, but let me put it this way George, I won't ask you not to do something that I do.'

The physician smiled gently again as he considered his own, rather fitting interpretation of the hypocrite's oath before adding, 'And who's Bernard by the way?'

▼

'That Dr Parkinson, he's a top chap, isn't he?' declared George with an agreeable nod of approval as he settled down heavily on the sofa at home next to his wife that same evening.

'I didn't know you were going see the doctor,' replied Gaynor.' You didn't tell me. Why did you go?'

'To ask his advice about having a few drinks at the weekend.'

'I gather he's told you to carry on regardless judging by the look on your face.'

'Not in so many words, but he kind of didn't disapprove either, not unlike Consultant Killjoy.'

'Did you mention going to Australia?'

'I did actually, and he was all for it. Said something about it being of medical value because it was something to look forward to.'

'That Dr Parkinson, he's a top chap, isn't he?' replied Gaynor.

TEN

'Bernard!…I need a word.'

George was shuffling around the kitchen/diner making a mid-evening cup of tea. The temptation to knock the lid off a chilled lager was huge, but it was Thursday which meant that the lure had to be resisted. George found solace in the belief that looking forward to some beery froth on his top lip the following evening could be of medical value. According to that great bloke Dr Parkinson anyway.

The rest of the family had gone to the cinema leaving George alone, a rare and valued privacy, but one that had merely served to double the temptation to break the mid-week temperance vow. However, overcoming even this was better than two hours of neck strain in a noisy, germ-ridden picture house testing his short attention span to the limit.

'Bernard!…I need a word.'

George repeated his call for the dog, heard not a chirrup, so walked through to the lounge with his cup of tea where Bernard was dozing on the rug in front of the gas fire, ignoring him completely.

George sat down and patted the cushion next to him.

'Right Bernard, come up on here on the couch with me. Yes, I know you're not really allowed to, but the boss isn't here, so get your four big fat paws up here and give me a hug. I won't say anything if you don't. And no moulting.'

Bernard opened one eye, looked at George patting the cushion for a few seconds before comprehension clicked in. He heaved his body off the rug, trudged across the carpet, lolloped up on to the sofa, placed his front paws across George's legs and licked his face.

'You big soft thing,' said George, gently rubbing the dog's ears and pulling him up close.

'Now listen carefully. Pay attention and no nodding off because this is important. You already know that I've got cancer, so as part of the treatment we're all going to Australia for a big holiday. However – and brace yourself for a big doggy dollop of bad news here Bernard – I'm afraid you can't come. Sorry mate. Believe you me Bernard if I could take you, then I would, but that Gaynor just refuses to give up her place. I've told her how much it would mean to you, but she just won't listen. I know, it's so inconsiderate of her.

'But perhaps you wouldn't like it out there anyway. The place is full of dingoes and didgeridoos and nearly all the blokes are called Corey. The good news is that you get to stay with Harry next door, and while we've gone, I've a got a very important job for you. A seek and destroy mission worthy of that 007 chap himself, success guaranteed to attract every fruity canine this side of the spoil heap. What's a female St Bernard called anyway, would she be, possibly, a St Bernadette? Anyway, I digress Mr Bond. The mission – should you choose to accept it – is this. There's a mass murderer on the loose, one that's wreaking havoc with my pansies and threatening to take out all my tomatoes in the glasshouse. The enemies are called vine weevils and they're chewing through roots, destroying the very parts needed for survival. Seek them out Bernard. Kill boy, kill.'

George paused, swallowed hard and looked forlorn as he stared up at the ceiling, his eyes brimming. 'What do vine weevils remind you of Bernard? Little killers eating away at the vital bits that keep you alive. Does that sound familiar to you?'

George buried his head in the deep fur around Bernard's neck and tears trickled down his cheeks.

ELEVEN

NASA – the National Aeronautics and Space Administration agency in America – operates within a system governed by a whole host of rules, regulations and guidelines.

One such decree stipulates that a potentially hazardous asteroid is more than 460 feet wide and passes within 4.7 million miles of the Earth's orbit. This allows for the vast majority of marauding asteroids to be ignored completely. There are, after all, millions of them out there in an unimaginably vast area of space and even one deemed remotely risky one is afforded a considerable safety margin.

Professional scientists monitor asteroid movements, but so do amateurs, amateurs like Maurice Berlingo who had once again felt the urge to share his discovery with someone more important than himself.

Professor David Emmerson had taken his call at NASA and, quite unusually, had handled it with a smaller dose of scepticism than usual. The computer co-ordinates for the area of cosmos where Maurice Berlingo claimed to have spotted the asteroid were vaguely familiar to the professor. Having assured that caller that he would investigate, he asked his computer all the right questions, and seconds later a million dollars' worth of software confirmed the previous sighting of a potentially rogue asteroid on the prowl in this particular part of deep space.

Professor Emmerson was impressed, but potential rogue asteroids were still common occurrences and the scientist decided to take an early lunch.

TWELVE

George Longworth knocked on his neighbour's front door and waited for Harry to answer.

There had been a time – admittedly a time that had existed long ago here in middle England – when Harry would have left the door off the latch and George would have strolled straight in, probably whistling tunelessly just to register his presence. Sadly, this no longer happened for reasons George didn't particularly want to think about.

Harry opened the door and ushered his welcome guest into the lounge. 'Beer?' he asked before pausing and adding uncertainly, 'it is Friday after all and it is nearly night time. Well, it's quarter past six.'

'Is it Friday?' replied George. 'I'd never realised.'

Knowing, knavish glances passed between the two friends followed by a brief silence made up of mutual understanding. Harry disappeared into the kitchen for an unfeasibly short period of time before returning and throwing a can of chilled beer across the room to the newcomer on the sofa. It was plucked out of the air left-handed then opened at once with fluent arm movements of outstanding dexterity. Harry, wholly impressed, settled down in the single armchair on the opposite side of the room and produced a whoosh of his own.

'Cheers,' cried George, raising his can aloft and taking a deep swig, eyes closed, sigh deep. But the reality failed to live up to the expectation. The beer tasted metallic and slightly unpleasant, a long way from the epicurean delight that George had so looked forward to. He considered the notion that it was a bad brew, but deep inside the truth nagged and hectored. He needed his brave face again and raised the beer can into the air, calling for a toast without actually drinking any more.

'Here's to foreign travel,' he cried.

'It's on then?' asked Harry.

'Australia here we come,' answered George. 'Brisbane or bust. Sydney or sink. Adelaide and, er…something else beginning with the letter A.'

'Armageddon?' chuckled Harry. 'When are you off anyway?'

'Easter,' replied George. 'It's a few weeks away yet and Gaynor's doing all the sorting, flight tickets, visas, hotel bookings, insurance, the whole nine yards. Apparently, you can do it all on the internet these days. I leave all that stuff to her and the kids. They all think I'm completely useless on a computer, which really bugs me because they're so right. I've only just mastered the remote control for the television and that's nearly ended up on the back of the fire a few times.'

Harry smiled and drank some more beer. He didn't complain about the taste.

'Anyway, I need a favour,' said George.

'Don't tell me, you want me to look after Bernard while you're away,' replied Harry.

'Correct and thanks for that my old mate, it's much appreciated by both of us, me and Bernard I mean. Bernard would hate it in kennels, he really dislikes most other dogs. He's not the violent type, but if he could ever catch that yapping terrier that lives at twenty-two, I feel sure we would have bloody carnage on our hands. The eyes give it away every time. Anyway, I've taken the liberty of informing Bernard of the preliminary plan, but we all need to talk it over in full. Hang on there, I'll go and get him.'

And with that George walk out through the front door leaving Harry on the sofa both bewildered and bemused.

George returned a few minutes later with a plodding Bernard by his side, the dog immediately opting for a quick snooze in front of the gas fire in most familiar surroundings. The rug in the Pickford household was, in his humble opinion, far more accommodating that the one back home. Bernard was no stranger to the neighbour's home. George often called in with him before and after walks and there was often a treat to be guzzled especially if Esme was cooking in the kitchen. This particular evening, he had to be content with a more comfortable rug tickling his tummy.

'Bernard's got used to more walks in the daytime since I had to give up work', said George. 'I realise this will be difficult for you because you still have a proper job, but don't worry about it. He likes a good snooze, some of them can last for hours, and a few snacks will always help him forget about a stroll around the spoil heap. He's got a bit of a sweet tooth as well these days. He's particularly fond of After Eight mints. Isn't that right Bernard?'

The dog lifted his right paw as if saying "yes" in complete understanding.

'I had him down as more of a Dairy Milk Tray type myself', replied Harry, struggling to maintain a straight face.

'What do you think of Dairy Milk Tray Bernard? Do you like them?' asked George.

The dog lifted its left paw.

Which meant "no".

THIRTEEN

'My dad says we're all going to die soon. It doesn't matter whether you live in America, England or Australia, we're all doomed.'

'He's said that before,' scoffed Larry. 'And we're all still here. Perhaps your dad would be better off with a new hobby. Don't you Americans all play golf?'

Larry was speaking to Michael Berlingo on Skype, an unreliable picture of his new transatlantic friend sporadically slipping in and out of focus on the screen of his laptop.

'This asteroid's carrying a hefty payload and it's heading our way,' chuntered the American accent, the voice also wavering and fluttering as the internet connection threatened to drop out completely.

'When and where is it going to crash into earth?' asked Larry.

'Not a clue,' replied Michael. 'Could be anywhere, but it doesn't really matter because we're all going to die anyway.'

'It might land on your house, thousands of miles away, so I'll be fine,' replied Larry.

'Not so my friend. If it does land here in the States, a huge tsunami will come racing across the Atlantic at about five hundred miles an hour and drown you all in your beds. Either that or the falling red hot rocks blasted into the air will set the world on fire and if that doesn't get you then the dust and debris in the atmosphere will blot out the sun for years which means nothing will grow and we'll all starve to death.'

'It's real good fun talking to you Michael, do you know that?' replied Larry. 'And anyway, how come no-one else is prattling on about the end of civilisation as we know it. You would think it might get a mention somewhere else.'

'My dad's right out in front with this one. He's told NASA about it, but they don't seem all that interested. I know he's been wrong before, but you never know, this time he might just be right.'

There was a knock on Larry's bedroom door and George walked in with a large mug of tea in his hand. He watched intently and listened curiously as an American voice behind a distorted young American face faded and fluttered on the computer screen.

'That's Michael, my friend in America. He's on Skype,' explained Larry.

'What's that then, some kind of hallucinogenic drug?'

Larry sniggered softly but managed to stop himself just before he started to speak. He was minded to hector his dad about his Luddite, technophobic ways and his apparent refusal to embrace the modern communication modes as frequented by cool dudes such as himself and his transatlantic buddy. But he had delivered similar polemics before to no avail, and in light of his father's burdening health problems decided enough was enough. Cancer had this way of maturing 16-year-olds wearing the clever trousers.

He smiled benignly and replied, 'No Dad, Skype is a name, a name for a computer communication device. Michael's on it now and he's telling me that an asteroid is heading our way and we're all going to die.'

'Well, we've all got to go one day,' replied George sullenly with an enigmatic shake of his head.

'I'll leave your tea on the bedside table.'

George turned and headed towards Katie's room. Again, he knocked on the door before being asked to enter. He reflected on how much time both his maturing children spent alone in their own bedrooms these days, usually hanging on grimly to some manner of electronic device with both hands. Katie slept with her mobile phone on her pillow, protestations from both parents brushed breezily aside. Is it ever good news if somebody rings at two in the morning?

'Hi hun', he said, perching uncomfortably on the edge of the single bed next to his horizontal daughter who reluctantly dragged her gaze away from the small screen.

'Hi Dad. I've been researching Australia and it's all looking good. Did you know that you can see the Great Barrier Reef from space?'

'Better pack my best pair of swimming togs then, just in case anybody's passing overhead aboard a Saturn rocket and looking down. What's this fascination with space anyway? Larry asked me what an asteroid is a few days ago. Then he told me that this American friend he talks to on Sky Sports has a telescope and is predicting that a huge asteroid is heading our way and that we're all going to die. What's all that about then?'

'It's Skype, not Sky Sports,' replied a giggling Katie. 'And it's his dad who's got a telescope, not him.'

'Whatever', replied George, getting further on down with the kids. 'Australia here we come then my little puff adder.'

'That's right. It's going to be a hoot dad.'

'Sure is,' replied George, heading for the door. He was fairly confident in his reply, but deep down he knew that two weeks without Bernard's sage counsel and companionship – especially when man and dog were in digs on different hemispheres – were going to be a big ask.

Part Two

FOREWORD

Nestling deep in indigenous Australian history, Aboriginal tradition maintains that sacred sites lie within the natural landscape and retain a special significance.

Hills, rocks, waterholes, trees, plains and other rustic features may be nominated sacred sites. In coastal and sea areas, these revered places may include locations which lie both above and below water. Sometimes sacred sites are obvious, such as natural earth pigment deposits, rock art galleries, or spectacular natural features. In other instances, sacred sites may be unremarkable to an outside observer. They can range in size from a single stone or plant, to an entire mountain range. Many, thanks to a lack of artificial light pollution, offer pilgrims a mesmeric view of the night sky and a stunning array of countless millions of glistening stars.

ONE

Jamal Jawai was rapidly becoming the darling of the National Rugby League in Australia. A title up against some pretty stiff competition. Especially for an Aboriginal.

Jamal's considerable physical presence and fabulous talent on the killing fields of Sydney, Brisbane and Melbourne were playing a big part in his burgeoning superstar status. State and international honours were surely only a matter of time. Meanwhile his dashing good looks and endless braided hair – tied back in a big man bun on big match day – were also proving to be irresistible newspaper and glossy magazine fodder. Television cameras had also fallen for his character and charisma and Jamal was pleased and proud to represent and dignify the indigenous people of his ancient homeland.

But today, his face perspiring and bloodied, he peered anxiously in the mirror to be greeted by the sight of two eyes blackening quickly either side of a badly broken nose dripping with blood.

The fearsome back row forward swept back his huge mane of black hair and swiped the many beads of sweat off his semi-naked, pulsating, massively muscled body before turning to his team mates who were lounging in various states of undress in a semi-circle of seats behind him.

'Still bloody good-looking though,' he growled, grinning inanely and looking around expectantly at his team mates for confirmation of his theory. He received a chorus of raucous jeers and hoots of light-hearted derision. Somebody threw a muddy, rolled-up sock at him. The atmosphere in the dressing sheds was a convivial blend of triumph and camaraderie born of a collective adversity, but Jamal had paid a high price for the buoyant mood of himself and his companions.

The Sydney Barracudas had courageously clung on to a 22-18 score line to grab a vital win over the Canterbury Cardinals in a particularly brutal rugby league affair at the city stadium. The final ten minutes had witnessed a stirring fightback from the Cardinals, one the Barracudas had resisted with considerable fortitude. There had been less than two minutes left on the clock when frustration had got the better of the Cardinals' hefty Samoan prop who decided to vent his emotions on Jamal's exposed head with an old fashioned and illegal stiff-arm tackle. The assailant was sent off, Jamal helped off aboard trembling legs with blood seeping from both nostrils.

Now he was recovering in the heady atmosphere of a winning locker room. Victory, as ever, was proving to be the ultimate anaesthetic.

The Barracudas' physio led Jamal into the treatment room and sat him on the bench.

'That nose is badly broken which means no rugby for you for a few weeks. You can have it fixed properly when you retire. They can get them nice and straight these days. The media want to interview you by the way. There's a television camera and crew waiting to pounce in the corridor outside. If I were you, I'd turn them down. They only want to film your smashed nose. Tell them it's not a freak show.'

'Talking to the media is important,' replied Jamal. 'Especially for guys like me.'

'How do you mean guys like you? Guys with two black eyes and a nose pointing east instead of north?'

Jamal cast the physio a disparaging look but carried on regardless. 'A guy like me because I'm an Aboriginal, not a guy looking for sympathy or sporting the spoils of war. We've spent years battling inequality and lack of opportunity in this country and success in sport is one way of fighting back. We need to put ourselves out there.'

The physio said nothing and looked uncertain. Jamal sensed his unease.

'Anyway, the media boys might offer me a job one day, especially when I've had my nose done which will mean I'll be even better looking than I am now. If that's possible of course.'

Jamal eased his aching body off the treatment bench and headed for the door. 'Where are you going?' demanded the physio. 'I've not even cleaned the dried blood off your face yet.'

'To talk to the media,' replied Jamal. 'The interviewer might be big Sam, one of the brothers.'

It was indeed one of the brothers. A grinning Sam Runceman was lurking with intent in the narrow corridor outside the treatment room, his huge frame almost filling the passageway. A fellow Aboriginal and recently retired professional rugby league player for city, state and country, Sam was a colourful, self-confident character as well as an admired television personality and interviewer. Hence, he was clutching a microphone and wearing a natty green blazer provided by the television company he was representing. He was also wearing a bemused half-grin as he took on board Jamal's smashed face.

'Jamal my poor lamb, what have they done to you? That broken nose means you're no longer better looking than me. This must be devastating news. Are you thinking of retiring and living in a cave in the Outback as a recluse?'

'I assume that thing is turned off,' replied Jamal nodding towards the microphone and smiling.

'Yes, but we're live on air in less than thirty seconds. Let's get that blood off your face. We need to look our best for the millions of our adoring fans out there.'

Sam pulled a handkerchief out of his pocket, moistened the corner of it with the tip of his tongue and dabbed delicately at the player's face. Jamal laughed, but didn't pull back or object. A cameraman and sound technician tucked themselves in either side of the interviewer's chunky shoulders. Sam placed an inquisitive finger on a communications device in his ear, nodded and mouthed, 'we're on... three, two, one... going live'. He thrust the microphone under the player's smashed nose and started to speak.

'Jamal my poor lamb, what have they done to you? That broken nose means you're no longer better looking than me.

This must be devastating news. Are you thinking of retiring and living in a cave in the Outback as a recluse?'

Jamal stared at Sam, eyes opened wide by the sheer audacity of the smirking man with the microphone in the midst of all manner of mischief. A raucous laugh was making its way up from the pit of his stomach, quite prepared to make itself heard live on national television. It just didn't care. The brain had lost control. The guffaw exploded from Jamal's lungs and runaway chuckles cascaded from his gaping mouth. Speech was impossible. Sam held his nerve for not too many seconds before the infectious laughter broke down his crumbling defences too. Both interviewer and player were giggling senselessly. A sporting nation joined in. Sam was the first to regain a measure of composure. He gasped, coughed, dabbed a tear of laughter from his eye and asked. 'So, Jamal what will you do with your time off with that broken nose?'

'Going back home to see Jenny and the family,' spluttered Jamal. 'And visit the sacred sites.'

TWO

Jamal Jawai had been born 23 years earlier in a poor and run-down Aboriginal village, the eldest of three siblings.

The family lived on the edge of the Outback, a settlement not a vast distance from towns and cities, or 'civilisation' as allegedly brought to the South Seas shores by the invading white settlers in the none-too-distant past.

A poorly-maintained playing field on the outskirts of the village had helped to rescue Jamal from an almost inevitable descent into alcohol and associated drug abuse as suffered by so many young men and adults in his community. It was one of the more responsible village adults who was to be his ultimate salvation. Jenny Moynahan, then in her mid-thirties, was appalled by the degradation and poverty pulling her community apart.

But one of the village youngsters gave her hope for the future. She would watch twelve-year-old Jamal kick an old rugby ball about in the heat and dust of the "sports" field and was struck by his superb athleticism and ability to control the ball. She also noticed that the young boy was blessed with a remarkable physical presence, already a foot taller and a not dissimilar distance wider across the shoulders than his peers. When the other boys in the village formed two makeshift sides, Jamal's tremendous physique meant he would run through, over and around opponents with ease. He also trained his magnificent body without coercion, often working with home-made weights before running miles through the bush, usually alone.

Jenny and her village contemporaries – especially those with roots embedded in rural areas – tried diligently to retain ancestral family values. But parents, and unfortunately the mother and father of young Jamal, were too often dispirited by hardship and in turn disinterested in the social and intellectual development of their children. Too much time had to be given over to the everyday slog of life, time swallowed up by poorly paid menial tasks just to put food on the table and pay the bills.

It was the more caring adults like Jenny who would try to maintain tradition and uphold standards of the past, take the youths for walks into the bush to learn of the old ways or to sit around a camp fire on the banks of the river at night to hear of their connection to land and water. To marvel at myriad stars in the heavens above in awe and wonder. But Jenny realised that star-gazing and discussing the meaning of life around the camp fire, however enjoyable, would not enable young Jamal to fulfil the potential she felt confident was locked within, yearning to be released.

So, she washed down the battered Holden parked at the rear of her modest home, got Jamal to push it down the dusty track to bump-start it, and with one intrigued youngster in the passenger seat beside her, set off to kick-start the sporting career of a young man surely destined for better things.

She had previously spoken on the telephone to one of the junior coaches at the Sydney Barracudas and had not found the going easy. Don Ferris rather impatiently explained that all parents thought that their kids were superstars in the making and that success demanded massive commitment and dedication.

Jenny rather patiently explained that she wasn't his mother, but still believed that the youngster bristled with talent.

'He's not very old, but he's already over six feet tall and fifteen stones,' she said.

'How old is he?' demanded Ferris.

'Twelve.'

'We don't have a league for players that young. The juniors start at sixteen and just because he's a good young one, doesn't necessarily mean he'll turn out to be a good older one. The other kids will catch him up eventually. We see that all the time.'

'Please let him train with and then play for the Under 16's insisted Jenny, rather taken back by her own audacity. 'Just once at least. I guarantee he won't let you down.'

'Four years is one hell of a leap up out of his age group for a kid of just twelve. Four years, jeez, it's never been known. I can't take any responsibility for his safety. No way, no, I can't allow it.'

'I'll take full responsibility for him,' replied Jenny, now suddenly nervous, aware that she was rushing headlong into uncharted territory and taking a big gamble she had not anticipated.

'You'll have to sign something to make it official. I'm not copping for any flak if it all goes wrong.'

'I'll sign anything you want, within reason of course,' replied Jenny.

Ferris scratched his head and replied reluctantly. 'Okay, bring him along on Saturday morning. The Under 16's have a training session and then a friendly against the Harriers. Well, when I say friendly…'

THREE

'Tell me again where we're going,' said Jamal as he clambered into Jenny's clattering, careworn car.

'Sydney. The training ground at the Barracudas. You're going to train with the Under 16's and then play for them.'

'The Under 16's? Won't they all be bigger than me?'

'There will be some players in the Under 21's who won't be as big as you,' replied Jenny with a confident smile.

'But this isn't just about size. I need you to show these guys how determined and talented you are. And more than anything you must stand up for yourself. Don't be intimidated or frightened. Be fearless. The colour of your skin means that some of the opponents will try to bully and humiliate you. This can't happen. You mustn't let it happen. Show them you're a man not a boy. Can you do this Jamal? God has given you great physical gifts my son, gifts that can lift you out of our drab village existence and lead to a far better life. You've seen the professional rugby league players on television, the lifestyles they lead, the money they're paid. But they work tirelessly for their rewards and you can guarantee that they have all trained hard and played hard ever since they were your age, possibly even younger. Success like that can never come easily. This is your big chance Jamal. Do you want to take it?'

Jamal was quiet and thoughtful as the car trundled off the country track and joined the dual carriageway that would take them into the city.

▼

The pocketful of interested on-lookers and parents taking on board the junior Barracudas' training session had no inkling that the new kid on the block was just that – a kid.

Ferris introduced the newcomer to the teenage players willing to listen but made no mention of the age difference. Jamal made no mention of the fact that he was the only Aboriginal on the park.

The session commenced and the stranger in their midst easily matched – and bettered – most of his older colleagues for physical size while he was more enthusiastic than many. He won two of the longer sprints and bench-pressed the weight of the scrum-half. Even Ferris was slightly impressed.

The players took a refreshment break after an hour's training then after a thirty-minute rest were called together under the posts by Ferris. The coach read out the team to face the Harriers with Jamal starting on the bench to replace one of the props after twenty minutes. Jamal had never played a properly organised game of rugby before. But despite his size, he knew he wasn't a prop.

The Harriers were a hefty set of well-developed, serious young men who gathered in a huddle shortly before the kick-off to demonstrate their collective dedication to the cause. The dedication continued after the kick-off, the visiting side dominating their opponents by dint of their sheer physical presence, particularly up front where their number eight – an arrogant youth called Wayne Mountain aptly enough – ruled, his massive frame causing the Harriers' front row all manner of grief.

After fifteen minutes of watching his pack being forced almost permanently on to the back foot, Ferris whistled to Jamal and shouted, 'Deboo time, Abbo.' The youngster flinched, but otherwise didn't react. Instead, he flexed the muscles he thought he ought to flex, placed the gum shield that Jenny had bought him over his top set and gave a small wave to his guardian angel who was standing on the opposite touchline stepping from one foot to the other. Jenny looked more nervous than he felt.

Jamal helped his side defend their own try line for a full set of six before the Harriers ran out of tackles and handed over possession deep in enemy territory. The weary Barracudas' half-back looked for a fresh runner and threw the ball straight to Jamal. The new kid sucked in a big lungful of air, picked up as much pace as possible in limited space and ran straight into the flailing bulk of a sneering Mountain. The callous prop hit his opponent straight in the face with his forearm, high, deliberately and illegally. Blood was already flowing as the ball was forced out of Jamal's grasp and he fell to earth, Mountain following his hapless victim all the way down with a vicious elbow to the back of the neck. The prop then lay on top of his stricken opponent and hissed in his ear, 'That's your career finished Abbo, now get back to your fucking mud hut.'

Jamal lay still for a few seconds to collect his mazy, muddled thoughts. He then pushed down on his immense arm muscles, forced his body upwards and thrust Mountain off his back. Jamal stood up and in his cupped right hand caught constant drips of blood pouring from his wrecked nose. Mountain scrambled to his feet and stood in front of him, smirking and gloating as the referee ran over. He was too late. Jamal drew back his fist and smashed Mountain in the face as hard as he could. He felt and heard the nose break and watched his opponent topple on to the rock-hard turf, an undignified mess.

There were angry shouts and threats and suddenly Jamal was fighting several opponents, new assailants rushing at him from all angles. He stood his ground, landing heavy punches and refusing to go down, refusing to give in, refusing to be bullied and insulted ever again. Some of his teammates ran over to join in as a mass brawl ensued at the end of which Jamal was still standing, blood still pouring, but no-one daring to hit him again. Mountain remained horizontal and moaning as a medic rushed to his aid.

On the touchline, Ferris shook his head slowly and muttered softly to himself, 'I knew something like this would bloody well happen.'

Behind him another voice sounded, startling Ferris, causing him to turn.

'Who's the new kid? He can't half look after himself. What a fight that was.'

The voice belonged to James Hollingworth, the Barracudas' chief executive, secretly watching the Under 16's on a scouting mission of his own.

'His name's Jamjar, or something stupid like that anyway. A trialist. He's only bloody twelve,' mumbled Ferris.

'Twelve!' exclaimed Hollingworth. 'What on earth... only twelve and he took most of them on single-handedly... sign him. Sort him with a junior contract.'

'Sign him?' replied an aghast Ferris. 'But he's a bloody Abbo.'

'Sign him,' retorted Hollingworth firmly. 'And those are my final words on the matter... apart from two more.'

'And what might those be?' scoffed Ferris.

'You're fired,' replied Hollingworth.

FOUR

It was to his ancestral home, the Aboriginal community which had helped him shape such a successful sporting career, that Jamal – now 23 years old – would return.

Once again, a broken nose was playing a big part in the events of his life, and once again, the unfortunate, rather painful injury was opening a door of opportunity. Jamal wanted to visit the village elders, his parents, his brother and sister, but more than anyone he wanted to see Jenny. His guardian angel had nurtured him through the fraught early years as he forged success and won over admirers in junior ranks at the Barracudas. She had driven him to training, spent countless hours on the touchline watching him train and play, offered him support and sympathy, tended his wounds, sustained his spirit.

She had been his constant companion and mentor until Jamal's independence had gradually come between them.

The club, tending to the needs of a player they realised was an exciting, long-term investment, had provided their protégé with a city apartment five minutes' walk from the training ground and a junior contract that handed him a comfortable living. Distant memory Don Ferris had been right about one thing, many youngsters at the club could now match him physically, but Jamal retained an aura, an innate strength which still stood him apart from the chasing pack.

Jamal had never lost contact with Jenny, even when he had broken through into the big time. He still drove to his village home to see her when he could, and she had cried when he proudly told her he had been named as club rookie of the year when he was just 17. Jamal had cried too. But now his latest broken nose was providing him with the opportunity to spend more than just a few hastily grabbed hours to visit the woman to whom he owed so much.

Jamal stopped his car in a cloud of dust outside Jenny's extremely modest home and peered anxiously at the faded and cracked front door. It opened almost immediately, and Jenny stepped out on to the verandah, a little older and a little less certain on her feet these days, but still possessed of a determined and confident spirit. She issued a cheery wave and smiled with admiration as Jamal hauled his massive frame out of the car, leapt up three wooden steps in one bound and took the mother he never really had into his arms. Jenny almost completely disappeared within his engulfing embrace. Tears were shared followed by more hugs, a pot of tea and sticky buns.

'I saw what that horrible player did to your nose and the television interview afterwards,' she said, chortling softly. 'Apparently it's one of the most watched clips on all those silly social media sites. I must admit it was funny though. That guy Sam Runceman is quite a character, isn't he?'

'He certainly is and he's one of us too,' replied Jamal. 'He does a lot for the sport and our people. I'd like a career in the media when I retire, just like the one Sam's forging for himself.'

'You'll have to get one of those internet things, make a name for yourself on Titter or whatever it's called.'

'It's called Twitter and I've already got an account,' chuckled Jamal. 'I mentioned on it that I was going to visit the sacred sites while I've got a couple of weeks off and that's caused quite a stir of interest. Many of my followers asked where the sacred sites could be found and what they meant to me.'

Jenny responded, 'I thought we could stroll down to the river this evening. It's a beautiful, clear night, the stars will be shining just like you shine Jamal. You're our shining star. You make us all feel so proud.'

Jamal blushed and sipped his tea.

▼

The shining stars were indeed in profusion.

Jenny and Jamal settled down together on a sandy shore on the edge of an oxbow lake by the side of the river and drank in the silence and serenity. A little too close for comfort, a menacing crocodile slipped almost silently into the sluggish grey water: a few yards further downstream a wary Blackbuck antelope slaked its thirst at the water's edge.

'This is one of our more ancient sites, stretching right back to the earliest years of our civilisation', said Jenny. 'It offers an unmatched view of the night sky and the boundless fascination that only Mother Nature can provide. Don't you agree Jamal?'

Jamal nodded his head and looked up at the heavens and the millions of stars above. Jenny moved closer to him and also peered into deep space before speaking.

'When you've studied the night sky for as long as I have, you learn to recognise the detail of the unchanging patterns, the countless objects that seem so close yet are so far away. Our ancestors believed that the day just one of those stars moved, broke away from its stable existence, then death and destruction would rain down on earth, taking much life, changing all life.'

There was a mutually comfortable silence as guardian angel and sporting protégé reflected on the spoken words before settling back into the peace and tranquillity the ancient site offered, a tranquillity rarely encountered by Jamal in the high-wire days of his dashing and demanding rugby league career.

Jenny continued to watch the night sky before suddenly stiffening and placing a hand over her mouth to stifle a gasp.

'One of the stars has moved,' she whispered ominously. 'It's not much, but its glorious light has been in the same place for more years than I care to remember and now it's different. It's not in the same place.'

Jenny pointed to the heavens and although Jamal followed her wavering finger it meant nothing to him. There were too many tiny flickering stars millions of light years away. Jenny sensed his bewilderment.

'You don't need to know which star it is, you will have to take my word for it.'

'What does it mean?' asked Jamal.

'Many of the tribal elders speak of the past, the distant past and the lethal forces that were unleashed from the heavens when the stability of the stars was lost. They talked of a huge, rogue asteroid causing fireballs to fall from the heavens, igniting vast tracts of the woodland and savannah, causing misery and chaos. Yet they recognised that this was an act of nature, not the wrath of the gods, and that the raging fires were responsible for an invaluable cleansing process on which our land grew to depend. The great infernos were part of a great renewal and not to be feared. They destroyed life yet also created new life and their legacy is the land that nurtures us today. The site where we seek solace tonight would not exist without them.'

Jamal was quiet for a while before speaking, 'So a fireball, a rogue asteroid, will fall from the heavens and everything will start to burn?' answered Jamal, wishing he could emulate the eloquence of present company.

'This is what our forebears always believed happened in the past and today modern science has proved them to be right,' replied Jenny.

Jamal thought about what he ought to do next and his mind turned to modern science.

▼

Jamal Jawai's Twitter following was in the thousands and counting.

His deliberations on world class rugby league were closely monitored and digested, but the sporting icon was also more than happy to opine and pontificate on social issues and world events. The imminent end of this very same world was possibly an event that would arouse the Twitterati. Jamal had always intended to enlighten his followers after his visits to the sacred sites, to tell of his ancestors' beliefs and customs, to help pay back the people who had provided him with the opportunity to reap so much from his celebrated lifestyle. They probably didn't expect to read that they were all going to die soon. But Jamal had much faith in Jenny – she had shown much faith in him – so he felt it only right that her reading of the stars inhabiting the night sky was deserving of public debate down on planet internet.

Sofa-surfing in his rather comfortable apartment, Jamal lit up his computer screen and loaded his Twitter page. He wanted to do justice to Jenny's beliefs and, after several minutes thought, typed: "The Aboriginal elders believe the night sky holds many secrets. They predict death and destruction will fall from outer space. A rogue asteroid is heading our way."

Jamal closed down his computer and went to bed. That would give them all something to get in a froth about.

▼

The Texan night sky was shrouded in thick cloud which meant Michael Berlingo was confined to his bedroom, attracted to his computer screen like a moth to a light bulb.

His father had continued to monitor the night sky and was still convinced that a massively destructive asteroid was heading the way of planet Earth. But once again supporting evidence was scant. His dad was either a wayward genius being ignored by those who ought to know better or he was wrong again. Michael was determined to find out which.

Official websites, including NASA's own offerings, proved to be barren hunting grounds as were searches for asteroid strikes. There had been many in the recent past, but none of any real significance and while there were several historical reports of near misses, few had attracted much attention. Michael sighed and started again. He decided on a random attack approach, pressed the keys to summon professor Google and typed in 'rogue asteroid.'

The good professor provided the usual myriad answers, the lead items mainly shock, horror newspaper stories, predictable members of the hand-wringing American press pushing the usual panic buttons. Michael scrolled down to try and locate more sober headlines and hopefully less frenetic journalism. He came across articles about how to stop an asteroid – or not as the case may be – the fortunate and protective barrier that Earth's own moon provides, and a track called 'Rogue Asteroid' by "The Subterraneans", leading purveyors of heavy rock music – how apt – doom, psych and toner tracks also available. Good old Google.

Then, even lower down the page, he happened upon a small article in an Australian newspaper which related the rather unusual story of a leading rugby league player – one Jamal Jawai – telling of how Aboriginal elders in the village of his birth are predicting that a rogue asteroid is heading towards the earth bringing with it all manner of death and destruction. The sage elders could make their prophecy of doom by merely sitting in the dust of a sacred sight and gazing up at the night sky just as their ancestors had done. Australia? Wasn't that where his English friend Larry Longworth was soon headed. Sure as hell was.

Michael decided he had better tell Larry that he had been right all along. He and his family were heading straight for big trouble.

▼

Jamal had also been right about one thing – his tweet had certainly given a lot of people an excuse to work up a lather and even some newspapers had reported his outlandish claims.

However, he was disappointed to learn that most comment was at best, sceptical, and at worst disparaging. Not a lot of credence was forthcoming, a response which underpinned Jamal's suspicions that even some of his more faithful Twitter followers still harboured a smidgeon of prejudice against the Aboriginal people, particularly the older generation. But then again, he could be wrong. Many of those cascading cold water on his rogue asteroid theory pointed out that no scientific boffins were pointing towards the heavens in alarm while using their other hand to dig an emergency underground bunker in their back gardens, complete with many tins of soup, a spare survival jacket and 12 months' back copies of "What Satellite" magazine.

Perhaps Jamal's next tweet had better stick to how long it would be before his broken nose was better.

Part Three

ONE

'That thing will never get off the ground.'

George Longworth and his family were standing next to a twenty feet high window, gazing in awe and admiration at the enormous Airbus A380 airplane glowering menacingly before them on the airport apron.

'That plane is bloody huge. How on earth does it get into the air?' asked George of anyone willing to listen.

'The wings on a fully loaded Airbus A380 can flex up to four metres on take-off', remarked Larry. 'Didn't you know that Dad?'

'Well, everybody knows that don't they?' interjected Katie with a snort of derision. 'Is that our 'plane by the way? The one we're actually going to fly to Australia on.'

'That's our baby,' replied George, 'Here to Bangkok, a night spent avoiding the flesh pots of that notorious city then a relatively short hop to Sydney. It will be a breeze. I do hope Bernard's going to be okay without me. I do hope I'm going to be okay without Bernard.'

▼

The journey was anything but a breeze. Nearly fifty long hours later, the Longworths hauled their weary bodies off the wide body of the jet that had been their enforced bivouac for far too long. It was mid-morning in Sydney and a stiff sea breeze pegged back the late summer temperature. Votes on what to do next were taken, baths, beds and bugger-all winning by a landslide. Opera houses, beaches and barbeques all lost their deposits.

The hotel of their choice was close to the sea front in the laid-back suburb of Manly, 17 kilometres north east of Sydney central. The impressive, white-topped, rolling waves and glistening beaches held no allure. The taxi dropped them outside their accommodation. An 'A' frame advertising hoarding standing in front of the hotel lobby promoted an imminent home game for the Manly Cormorants in the NRL. Some wild-haired bloke called Sam Runceman stared out at them from the poster sponsored by a national television network. 'Sam the Man' was clutching a microphone and wearing a natty green jacket and a large, inane grin.

'That's rugby league that is,' remarked Larry, dumping his suitcase unceremoniously on the decking and pointing at the advert. 'It's supposed to be big over here. Some of the star players are national celebrities, just like our footballers back home, but with only one hairdresser.'

No-one was listening. 'It's half past ten in the morning and to avoid jet lag we really ought not to go to bed right now. That's the theory anyway,' said Gaynor.

'We all need some proper sleep, at least I do, desperately,' yawned George. 'We'll have a few hours shut-eye and then go out this evening for an explore and a few scoops which will mean bedtime at the right time. I always thought jet lag was made up by wimps who just couldn't keep up the pace. I now know differently. Someone grab that receptionist. I yearn for a mattress.'

TWO

Larry dozed intermittently for a few hours in his rather pleasant Manly hotel room.

Despite feeling fatigued, he was also slightly disorientated which meant sleeping in the afternoon felt strange and difficult to achieve, despite his father's many complaints about the amount of time his son spent prostrate on his bed back home, "not being productive."

He pushed back the duvet, clambered out of bed, dragged his laptop from his unpacked suitcase and opened it on the glass-covered table in his room, pulling up a cane-backed chair as he did so. He clicked on the Skype icon at the side of the screen and noticed that he had a missed call from Michael Berlingo in Texas. He was about to reply when he suddenly thought about the time difference. It was 2.00pm in Sydney and after consulting professor Google for help, discovered that he was 15 hours ahead of his American friend. He closed his eyes, thought hard and wished he had paid more attention in maths lessons. So that made it 11 o'clock at night over in the States. Did it? Was he right? He was about to find out.

Larry clicked and pushed the buttons he needed to, and Michael's face appeared on the screen.

'Still alive then?' sniggered the familiar American accent.

'Barely, after that awful flight. And as for that stop-over in Bangkok – I won't be returning there in a hurry.'

'You won't be returning at all, because we're all going to die horrible deaths in a terrible inferno that will engulf the earth and destroy every living plant and animal. Even cockroaches will be wiped out which would be a real bonus. It's just a shame that we won't be here to appreciate it.'

'Lovely to speak to you again Michael, so uplifting as usual,' replied Larry. 'A few words with you and life feels truly worth living. So, I'd better be making the most of the ten minutes or so I've got left here on the planet. I assume the killer asteroid has bought the duty-frees, left the departure lounge and has been cleared for blast off, destination planet Earth.'

'You may scoff my English buddy, but my dad's sure about this one. The asteroid is heading our way and there's no way out. You've tried to escape to Australia – my dad's from Australia originally you know – but running away won't work. Death and destruction will be global. We've all got two weeks to live.'

'I've come here because my dad's dying of cancer', replied Larry quietly. 'But hopefully he's got more than two weeks to live.'

There was a brief, but awkward radio silence. 'Apologies,' mumbled Michael. 'Didn't know that. My mum died from cancer five years ago and it still makes me feel sad. Perhaps you'd just better get on with enjoying yourselves and forget about gloom and doom-merchants like me…' Michael's voice trailed off, mired in hesitancy and uncertainty.

Larry sighed and said. 'Sorry to bring us both down, but this trip is about my dad and the family and we need to make the most of it.'

'I'll speak to you again when you're back home in England,' replied Michael, his tone hushed. 'Take care of yourself and take care of your old fella. Just forget about the asteroid. My Dad's probably got it wrong again, so you just enjoy your time together and live the holiday to the full. As they would say in Australia, "no worries mate".

'No worries mate,' replied Larry, wincing at his wholly woeful attempt at an Australian accent.

'Speak to you soon.'

THREE

George struggled to sleep as well.

He stirred after a handful of fitful hours barely refreshed and didn't feel particularly chipper but put that down to the physical and mental turmoil inflicted during the previous two days spent gallivanting half-way around the world. He prodded a snoring Gaynor gently in the ribs and indicated that they ought to get out of bed. It was late afternoon and George figured that a bite to eat followed by a few tinnies of the amber nectar might serve them well and hopefully normalise a few wayward body clocks.

'Give Bill and Ben a ring on the internal phones. Tell them we'll all meet in the foyer in twenty minutes. Tell Larry it's his round and no, he can't have a lager. He's not old enough. I'm going to take some more of that bloody awful medication and have a shower.'

Twenty minutes later and the Longworth clan formed in orderly rank at the hotel bar, George running an inquisitive eye along the lager array before placing his order with a barman who looked like a young Pat Cash. It would not take George long to realise that a lot of Australians looked like a young Pat Cash. Even some of the women. George sipped his drink and winced slightly. One again it tasted metallic, a long way from toothsome. The enemy within did not recognise George's need to enjoy himself. Abnormal cell growths did not appreciate they were on the trip of a lifetime.

George produced a sad shake of his head and handed his drink to Larry who, although taken aback, consciously restricted his reaction to the slight raising of one eyebrow. He then glanced quickly from side to side and guzzled the lager noisily and gratefully before anybody changed their minds. But like his mother, he was surprised and slightly concerned. He had never known his dad give his beer away before. He had certainly never given it to Larry before. Gaynor frowned and looked at her husband, but decided it wasn't the right time to create a fuss. If there ever would be a right time. 'Come on', she said, 'let's go for a walk', somewhat reluctantly guzzling her own lager.

The family made their way on foot along the promenade and cycle track, alongside high-rise hotels, low rise surf shops and fast food shacks, beneath swirling, yapping seagulls all desperate to swoop on a stray hot chip. Joggers, strollers and cyclists hustled and bustled. Bedraggled surfers made their way off the beach after a long day catching the rays and rollers and trying to impress the girls.

George spotted a bar called the "Paralytic Parrot" and, vaguely amused, led in the troops, announcing that he was going to try a glass of wine as he did so. Katie and her mum said they would have one too in support of their father. Larry sensed the collective attention turn to him, so he dragged in a sharp intake of breath and asked for another lager. George sensed the presence of impudence, cast his son a knowing look and ordered the drinks as requested.

They settled in a corner of the rather raucous bar, George sampling his wine barely before his backside had hit the wicker. It tasted okay. George was pleased and smiled. Larry sensed his day of unwanted alcohol donation was already at an end. George raised his glass in the direction of his gathered kith and kin and proposed a toast. 'Here's to a fantastic holiday,' he proclaimed. 'What are we doing tomorrow?'

Two siblings and mother glanced at each other nervously. Katie seized the initiative. 'Me, you and Larry are all booked in to do a bungee jump. Off a big bridge over a big river up the coast. It's a surprise. Mum's already decided it's not for her, but she's still coming along for the ride. So, are you okay with that Dad?'

'Fair bloody dinkum I am!' exclaimed George in a wholly unconvincing Australian accent that was even worse than Larry's.

'Bring it on.'

But he downed his wine in one and wished he could talk to Bernard about this one.

'What does fair bloody dinkum mean?' asked Larry.

FOUR

The first full day of their holiday dawned fair and dry. Gaynor had organised a hire car to be dropped off in the basement car park of their hotel and after a substantial buffet breakfast, they picked up the keys at the reception and located the slate grey station wagon in its temporary subterranean home. Gaynor drove. George settled in the front seat and fiddled with the sat nav on the dashboard. Frustration and fretful tuts followed in seconds.

'It doesn't matter Dad. I've got the directions on my 'phone,' piped up Larry from the back. 'We head up on the coast road towards Brisbane in Queensland. It's a massive country Australia you know.'

They hit the long road ahead, the rather splendid coastal scenery a welcome bonus as the Longworth posse headed north to partake of an adventure that was now taxing minds both young and old, not least George's. As the family sped along in an unusually subdued mood, George tried to mentally cast aside his worries about his medical condition, not least the ramifications – and indeed wisdom – of plummeting head first down a steep ravine with a bit of rope attached to his ankles. However, he was determined not to let the enemy within inflict restrictions on his audacious adventure in this glorious land of opportunity and daring.

But George's trepidation about the bungee jump refused to be banished from his bustling brain. His thoughts enveloped and embraced it. Fretful fears hectored and nagged. He sensed his quiet family were reluctant to discuss the escapade that lay ahead because they suspected Dad was worried about it. He would show them.

'I assume they provide you with a rope when they lob you off this bridge,' he suddenly announced. 'Where exactly does it fit?'

'It goes around your neck,' sniggered Larry, which was arguably a typically mischievous response from an impudent 16-year-old languishing in the cheap seats.

'Larry!' Gaynor exclaimed. 'I really don't think that joke was in very good taste.'

But her attention was quickly taken by George in the adjacent seat who was chuckling softly to himself and making strange clucking noises. 'He's obsessed with death is that lad. It's not that long ago he told me a killer asteroid from outer space was going to see us all off and now I've got a noose round my neck as I leap head-first off some towering bridge towards certain death. It's a good job I've got a fantastic sense of humour with that macabre bugger chirping away in the background.'

'It's not a rope though is it?' interrupted Katie. 'It's a kind of thick elastic band which wraps around your ankles and then pulls you back up before any damage is done. Apparently, if they judge it just right, you can just dip your head in the river just before the elastic kicks in and saves you from being smashed to bits.'

George managed a brave smile and said, 'Looking forward to it more than ever Katie. Thank you for those few kind words of re-assurance.'

The car cruised on, past soaring cliffs, crashing surf and glimpses of beautiful beaches, temptations which needed to be overlooked as they surged onwards to their ultimate destination and an encounter with a death-defying plunge.

'What's this bungee place we're going to called again?' asked George.

'Jump the Shark', replied Larry.

'What…there are bloody sharks in the water!' exclaimed George.

'Only joking dad. Sharks don't live in this river…they've all been eaten by enormous crocodiles.'

George again took in a sharp inhalation of breath to deliver a second protest about crocodile-infested waters, but paused and took a few seconds to reflect before he nodded and said, 'That Larry's taking the piss, isn't he? And I don't think my darling daughter is a long way behind him. Are we even going on a bungee jump or is all this just an elaborate wind-up at my expense?'

'They are taking the pi…er mickey,' replied Gaynor, placing a reassuring hand on her husband's knee. 'But only to a certain extent. We are heading for a bungee jump, but it's only a small one, about a 40-metre drop and you can do it in tandem with an instructor if you prefer. Are you feeling less nervous now?'

'What made you think I was nervous? I'm fine with it and I'm going to do it on my own. But have you packed me a spare pair of Speedos just in case?'

FIVE

The meet-and-greet teenager at the bungee jump was everything George imagined he would be. Katie thought he was a bit of a dish.

A tangled mass of tatty, half-blonde hair – patently dyed – was partly piled up high in a bun on top of his head, his forearms were sinewy, sunburnt and tattooed while a scraggly, careworn beard framed a permanently gleeful grin. He was wearing frayed, cut-off jeans, flip-flops and a t-shirt emblazoned on the front with the motto: "Life is not a rehearsal." As the teenager strode purposefully towards the Longworths, he turned to deliver a volley of half-hearted insults at a nearby colleague who was wrapping thick, brightly coloured elastic rope into a coil. The back of his t-shirt read: "Daring before dementia." George just knew he would call them guys.

'Hi guys,' announced the happy hippy. 'I'm Dylan. It's

not my real name, but that's what you can call me. All the other guys do.'

'Hi Dylan', purred Katie. 'Nice tats. I'll bet you're a great surfer as well.'

Gaynor felt the need to wrest control. She sensed George was bristling and Katie was flirting. She was right on both counts.

'We're the Longworths from England. We booked on-line quite a few weeks ago and you emailed to confirm.'

Dylan reluctantly dragged his gaze from a pouting Katie, pulled a piece of paper out of his back pocket and scanned it briefly.

'Oh yeah, here it is, three Poms at three o'clock. Plenty of water in the river today. We haven't sent anybody crashing head first into the rocks since last Wednesday and that was only because it was my day off.'

Katie giggled nervously and blushed. George scowled.

Gaynor grasped the lead and the local lingo. 'Are there any medical conditions that would prevent any of these guys going ahead with the jump?'

Dylan looked straight at George who glared straight back at him before Queensland's Mr. Haircut pulled a second piece of paper from his other pocket.

'Right guys, I have a list of medical conditions here. Let me know when I get to one we need to know about. Have any of you ever suffered from, or currently have any of these little darlings? High blood pressure, heart condition, neurological disorders, epilepsy, previous dislocations, artificial limbs, asthma or pregnancy.'

Silence descended. No mention of cancer. George didn't know if he felt relieved or not. If he had been looking for a cop-out, there wasn't one available, although he had to privately admit that he wasn't too sure exactly what a neurological disorder was.

'All good to go then, Dylan me old mate. Three Poms to the slaughter,' chirruped George. 'I'll take off the old wooden leg when I get up there on the top stage.'

Dylan narrowed his eyes but didn't respond.

The "top stage" was attached to the side of a metal girder footbridge spanning a steep-sided gorge. It was a plank and scaffolding arrangement with an open platform to the front. The stage, directly overlooking the wide, sluggish river below, contained the anchor to which the coiled elastic bungee rope was attached. Access was via a long metal stairway up which the Longworth party duly made its way, Katie leading the ascent with a bound and the occasional quick step, George slightly more leaden-footed.

Dylan was already up there, stepping excitedly from foot to foot and dragging his long fingers through the thicket mess masquerading as his hair. But he quickly abandoned much of his head in the clouds persona to deliver a somewhat solemn diatribe about several safety aspects of bungee jumping, how to nose-dive off the platform correctly and how those taking part should generally disport themselves. He checked they had insurance and explained that the rope would stop bouncing with its passenger dangling not far from the surface of the water. This would allow two of his colleagues – Spider and Spudgun – to pick them up in a small rowing boat, detach the rope and take them to dry land. The landing pier, he was happy to inform them, was only a short walk from the club's own bar where the fortunate guests could re-live the thrill of their lives while blowing the froth off a few schooners of the old golden fluid. George pardoned the free advert and allowed Dylan to grow on him. A bit.

'Right guys, who's first?'

George, Larry and Katie looked at each other. Feet shuffled nervously, but then Katie took a confident step forward.

'Hi Dylan honey. I'm Katie and you can strap me straight in no worries. Where does the rope go? Do I need to take my jeans off?'

Dylan paused and smiled before telling her it was a pity, but that wouldn't be necessary. Katie blushed for the second time in a matter of minutes. Dylan led Katie to a set of scales at the side of the platform and weighed her.

'Now we know your weight, we can measure the bungee rope exactly so at the bottom of the plunge you dip your head into the water before it kicks in. We call it the baptism. Fancy it?'

Inwardly, Katie was petrified, but Dylan was looking particularly gorgeous close up. She cast caution to the wind and told him to go for it. Dylan carefully measured the rope, secured it to size on the anchor point then picked up a large towel from a pile stashed at the side of the platform. He double wrapped the towel around Katie's ankles followed by the rope tied over the towel with a series of elaborate knots. He pulled Katie to her feet by placing his hands around her waist, gave her an unnecessarily big hug and helped her shuffle awkwardly to the edge of the platform overlooking the 40-metre plunge to the water below. She looked down and her heart went from a loud thump to a tumultuous crashing against her rib cage. She wasn't sure if the palpitations were the result of the close encounter with Dylan or the thought of what she was about to do next. At the back of the platform, family members offered various vocal levels of support. Dylan said, 'Don't look down, look straight ahead. Lift your arms up, reach slightly forward then slowly let yourself fall, aiming outwards and head first. But before you go, you'll need this.'

Dylan slipped a small piece of paper into the back pocket of her jeans.

'What was that?' asked Katie.

'This bungee jump will be the second greatest thrill of your life. The piece of paper I've put in your back pocket is the ticket for the greatest thrill of your life.'

'What's on it?'

'My mobile number.'

"Smooth-talking bastard," thought Katie, but she allowed herself a smug little smile, leaned forward, lifted her arms and toppled off the edge of the platform into the void below without a care in the world. Dylan grabbed the safety rail at the side of the platform and watched Katie plunge. The top of her head just touched the water before the elastic cable pulled her to safety. Dylan waited until the bouncing girl had come to a standstill, watched Spider and Spudgun lift her safely into the boat and started to haul up the rope.

'Next,' he said.

George and Larry looked at each other and dad thought his son looked pale.

'You go Dad,' said Larry. 'Show this young lad of yours what you're made of.'

Gaynor added words of encouragement from the back.

George diverted his gaze to Dylan who pushed his mass of hair roughly into place and waved a beckoning arm, indicating that George should join him in the preparation area. Dylan proceeded with the same routine, but only after George had informed him that he didn't want to be ducked head first. He explained that he had just washed his hair and didn't want to ruin it. Dylan smiled weakly, not sure whether this rather enigmatic Pom was joking or not but adjusted the bungee rope according to his client's wishes. Fully strapped in, George shuffled warily to the edge of the platform.

George knew he shouldn't look down but couldn't resist. Forty metres looked like forty miles. He imagined he was staring down a gaping pit plummeting down to the depths of Hades. His head pounded with blood as his heart pumped wildly. When he had originally been diagnosed with cancer, George believed that nothing else in the world could terrify him more. Now he realised he'd been wrong. On the edge of the abyss with a beefed-up elastic band wrapped around his ankles, he couldn't believe how terrified he felt. His life lay in the hands of a hirsute, hapless hippy with dubious designs on his arm. And dubious designs on his daughter. But he quickly reasoned, was there a safer pair of hands back in that bloody cancer hospital back home? George closed his eyes and summoned every drop of courage his ailing body could muster. He raised his arms, vaguely latched on to a few words of reassurance from a purring Dylan, closed his eyes and toppled forward, feeling the adrenaline surge followed by the roaring wind rush through his perfectly washed hair.

'Next'.

Dylan had watched George pulled to safety in the muscular arms of Spudgun, so he yanked up the rope and turned to the youth who was the last to jump. He too thought he looked pale. Make that ashen. Larry dithered and turned to his mum who gave him a hug and a kiss.

'Dad and Katie will be waiting in the bar. Dad will probably let you have lager.'

Larry looked on anxiously as Dylan went through the preparation routine. He didn't ask if Larry wanted the baptism. He already knew what the answer would be. Larry shuffled along following in the scrape marks of father and sibling to the edge of the platform. By his side, Dylan was making all manner of reassuring noises. None of them entered Larry's overheating brain. In front he saw only light and sky, below he saw only certain death. He turned to Dylan and whispered, 'Can't do this mate.' He didn't even manage a woeful Australian accent.

Dylan slipped into well-rehearsed patter, 'It's okay to get nervous mate, quite normal. We see it all the time.'

'Not nervous at all. Absolutely petrified. Can't do it.'

'Sister and dad are already in our bar sinking a few schooners. You could be with them in minutes if you take the short cut straight ahead.'

'Absolutely petrified. Can't do it mate. Get my mum.'

Larry turned to his mum who was already hurrying to his side.

SIX

George, feeling rather pleased with himself, nestled down behind a brace of large lagers on a polished pinewood corner table in the 'Buck Stops Here.'

The bar walls were decorated almost entirely with photographs of various sportsmen and celebrities in various stages of bungee jump action. So, NRL heroes were to be seen grinning widely before the leap, beaming broadly during the leap and then chortling heartily as they shared the experience with an excitable Dylan and obliging bar staff after the leap.

George was also beaming broadly, but at his daughter who was sitting opposite nursing a tall flute of chilled sparkling wine. Her beam matched her dad's, but not for the same reason. George wallowed in his own thrilling sense of achievement. A warm fug of smug enveloped and caressed him and he allowed its tendrils to infiltrate his every sensory part. On this occasion he just knew the lager would taste right, ensuring a joyous celebration of victory against the unseen, malevolent enemy.

'I don't know about you my girl, but jumping off that bridge was bloody great,' he trilled. 'I was scared to death up there on that platform and to be honest I thought I was going to die on the way down. But now I'm here, alive, in one piece, it's got to be one of the best experiences I've ever had in my life. How about you, my little cuddly koala?'

'Wasn't Dylan so kind and reassuring? He made me feel so confident and relaxed. I really don't think I could have done it without him by my side.'

George raised a querulous eyebrow but maintained his silence.

'Two beers Dad?' quizzed Katie. 'Celebrations a bit thorough?'

'One of the lagers is for that underage hero son of mine. Could I have done that bungee jump at sixteen? I think not.'

'Perhaps you're more of a hero Dad. At your age and with, well, how shall we say, your spot of bother, and, er, how old exactly are you anyway?'

George was about to berate his daughter about her lack of family knowledge, but decided it was neither the time nor the place. It must be his good mood after his daring death-defying dive, one he had accomplished with such dash and élan. He checked his watch and looked across at the bar door. 'Your mum and brother will be here soon. They must have got Larry in the boat by now. I wish they'd hurry, I want to toast our successful adventure with the full squad as it were.'

George had barely completed his words when Gaynor and Larry pushed open the door. There was no sign of a spring in their steps. The shared gait was a worrying blend of a trudge and a slump. George leapt to his feet clutching then raising a lager in each hand, but even before he reached peak height, he realised all was not as it should be.

'I think hearty congratulations all around are in order', he cried. 'But…are they?'

'Larry didn't do the jump. He didn't feel very well,' gushed Gaynor.

'Thanks for the offer of an easy way out mum,' mumbled Larry sheepishly. 'But the truth is that my bottle went good style and it's me who needs the spare Speedos dad. Sorry family.'

SEVEN

The long car ride back to Manly was undertaken in a mostly uneasy silence, the views down to the crashing surf and early evening sun-dappled beaches somehow now not quite so appealing.

The mobile telephone number in Katie's back pocket was burning a hole in her jeans. She had already removed the slip of paper, read it several times, memorised it, put it back, and was tempted to ring the number. But two reasons prevented her. Firstly, she didn't want to seem too keen, and secondly, she didn't want to speak to the gorgeous one in the company of her nearest and dearest, all of whom were far too close for comfort. She checked the piece of paper was firmly nestled in her back pocket and opted to day-dream instead.

Despite Larry's attack of extremely cold feet, the bungee jump had been deemed a remarkable success and no-one had felt inclined to beat up Longworth junior. Lager and sympathy had been the orders of the day in the "Buck Stops Here". In normal circumstance, Katie might have been tempted to throw a couple of cheap shots at her younger brother after his obvious failings, but the circumstances were not normal. Better to make more of a fuss about her dad's heroics in the face of adversity. Besides, she had far more pressing matters on her mind, number one being most unexpected and promising encounter with the desirable Dylan. He had told them Dylan wasn't his real name. She wondered what it was and couldn't wait to find out.

It was late evening when the Longworths arrived back at their Manly hotel. Gaynor parked the hire car in its underground bunker and the members of the family retired to their respective bedrooms for an early night after the exertions of the day.

Larry lay on the bed and reflected on his new-found fear of free-falling from dizzy heights. He decided it wasn't worth fretting about and switched on the television which was fixed to the wall opposite the end of the bed. He flicked through several channels containing mainly nonsense and far too many adverts before happening upon a magazine programme about Australia's most popular sport, rugby league.

A large group of presenters – men and women – were sitting at the back of a large semi-circular table to form some kind of debating panel in front of a packed studio audience. Larry continued to watch and, as the camera panned across the set, he thought he recognised a familiar face.

Near the end of the line-up was a rather nattily-dressed Aboriginal man with big hair, wide shoulders and an even wider grin. Larry frowned, leaned forward and peered intently at him. Then one of the female presenters asked "Sam the Man" what he thought... and Larry had it. He was the television personality featured on the "A" frame advertising poster at the front of the hotel. He seemed to recall that his full name was Sam Runceman.

Sam the Man was sitting alongside another large and impressively muscular Aboriginal man. He too was operating somewhere beneath a thicket of black hair, braided and swept back. He was younger, less formally dressed and good-looking, despite the fading black and yellow colourations lingering around both eyes, legacies of a recent broken nose which was also still in evidence. Larry correctly assumed that the second guy was a leading NRL player carrying the spoils of war who was a guest for the evening.

The general tone of the studio debate was light-hearted, featuring footage of mistakes from the weekend games and street interviews conducted by a chap wearing a mankini which all and sundry seemed to find hilarious. Larry thought it rather distasteful. Then Sam the Man was handed the microphone and half-heartedly attempted a serious face. With the jaunty wave of an arm, he introduced Jamal Jawai – before immediately informing everyone that his guest needed no introduction – adding that his fellow giant indigenous had some grave, literally earth-shattering news to impart.

'Isn't that right Jamal?'

Jamal nodded and looked knowingly at his interviewer. He suspected Sam was about to have a right old guffaw at his expense.

'Jamal reckons that we're all going to die very soon, blown to smithereens by a large asteroid which is heading our way from outer space. We're all going the way of the dinosaurs, misery, suffering, and death followed by total extinction. Jamal's not even going to have time to get his nose fixed up, isn't that right mate?'

Jamal smiled sheepishly and thought about the high price of fame.

'Here are his own words, written after he had stared up into the stars and predicted a future which contains only complete and utter obliteration for us all,' added Sam, ratcheting up the hyperbole and knavery in equal measure. Sam paused, turned, and on a large screen behind them appeared Jamal's earlier tweet writ large and loud: "The Aboriginal elders believe the night sky holds many secrets. They predict death and destruction will fall from outer space. A rogue asteroid is heading our way."

Sam swivelled to face the audience. 'Surely the fireball from hell lurking in outer space can't hit us before the first State of Origin game? And what about the Grand Final? Nearly all the tickets have been sold.'

The camera panned to the audience who were in gales of laughter.

Jamal knew he just needed to go along with the huge joke that Sam and his co-conspirators were making of his now very public pronouncement. He reasoned it was better to play ball with the banter and let Sam entertain and amuse his audience, even if it was at his own expense. One day he might be doing the very same thing. But he quickly decided that he needed to keep Jenny out of it. He could explain why to his mentor later.

'So how exactly did you come up with this killer asteroid theory, my little Albert Einstein?' Sam warbled.

Jamal, now wrong-footed, hesitated, cleared his throat and prepared for more ridicule. But before he started to speak, Sam interjected. 'Did you look up at the night sky shortly after you'd taken that bang to the head, the one that broke your nose and ruined your good looks? Were you concussed my old mate? Dazed and confused?'

Jamal looked quizzically at Sam and suspected he was offering him an escape. He took it.

'It was after that bad knock, yeh. And I failed the concussion test in the sheds. Rough old game that rugby league isn't it?'

Sam nodded in agreement, looked straight into the camera and produced a knowing look and an impish, lop-sided grin, facial expressions that proclaimed: "mystery solved."

Back in the hotel room, Larry looked on in complete amazement. A random flick of the television remote followed by an interview with a popular sportsman would appear to be adding a serious layer of credence to the impending disaster theory so enthusiastically promoted by one Michael Berlingo and his mad dad on sky-at-night manoeuvres in their junior Jodrell Bank set-up somewhere in down-town Texas. He couldn't quite believe what he'd just seen and heard.

Larry diverted his attention back to the television and listened in amazement to wide-eyed, wide-shouldered, wide-boy Sam Runceman smirking that everything would be fine as long as the asteroid wiped out Adelaide first. The audience fell about the place.

Larry pressed the television off button and went straight on to Skype to speak to Michael Berlingo and hit him with some startling, yet possibly welcome revelations. His American friend appeared on the screen after only a few seconds. He expressed surprise that Larry had contacted him during his family holiday Down Under.

'I have to tell you about what I've just seen on television!' exclaimed Larry breathlessly. 'This Aboriginal guy, I think he's a professional rugby league player or something like that, was a special guest on this programme. He'd tweeted that his tribal elders have looked at the night sky and predict that a big asteroid is off course and heading to earth. That's exactly what your dad is predicting. So, he's not the only one who believes this is actually going to happen. Perhaps you're right after all.'

Michael paused and thought briefly before replying, 'You know, I think I've read a newspaper article on Google about this same Australian sports guy and what he's been saying. Yep, I remember now. Sure, it must be the same fella. I was going to tell you about him the last time I was in touch, but when you mentioned your dad and his illness, I didn't bother. But it's good to see that somebody else is taking this seriously.'

'The trouble is that no-body else apart from this guy does seem to be taking it seriously,' Larry pointed out. 'This poor chap, I think he's called Jamal, appeared on some manner of sporting magazine programme and basically they were all laughing at him and taking the piss. He ended up admitting that he's recently taken a knock to the head and I think he used this as a bit of a way out. It all seemed a bit bizarre if I'm being honest.'

Larry paused and added, 'So what do you think we should do now?'

'I think you ought to get in touch with this guy and pronto. Reply to his tweet, explain about my dad's theory and see if he bites. Did you say he's some kind of celebrity? You never know, you might even get to meet him. You might get on the television as well.'

'Are you serious?' gasped Larry.

'Go for it buddy, you never know. How's your dad by the way?'

'He's okay, pretty good actually. He did a bungee jump this afternoon, despite his condition.'

'That's so great. Did you do it as well?' asked Michael.

At this point, the screen flickered, jumped and went all fuzzy apart from a message which flashed up in the middle… connection lost.

Larry marvelled at how fantastic technology could be.

EIGHT

Katie was also horizontal on her bed, passing her mobile phone from hand to hand and planning her next move.

She felt more nervous than she had done standing on the brink of the bungee jump platform earlier that day, smiling slightly to herself when she considered that it was Dylan who had filled her with such confidence then, yet it was the same person who was filling her with such trepidation now. So many questions raced through her mind and had done so all the way up the coast road. Did he live at home with his parents? Was she up against a phalanx of fellow female admirers? Had he sneaked his phone number into her back pocket a bit of a jape – or even a bet – knavish ruses he could share with his chuckling mates over a few beers later that evening?

She had to cast such doubts and hectoring thoughts from her mind and there was only one way to achieve this –

ring him. She mentally muscled up, breathed deep and hard, gripped the phone firmly in one hand and hit the buttons. She didn't need to consult the piece of paper.

The ring tone rang out, her heart fluttered and almost without delay, Dylan was in her right ear. He was purring again.

'Hi honey,' he drooled. 'How's my little pomme de terre?'

Pomme de terre? thought Katie. Isn't that French for potato? This guy's either trying too hard or he's as thick as a set of cork mats. Or drunk. Or stoned. Or all four. Katie decided she'd better give the gorgeous one the benefit of the doubt so early in the equation.

'Don't you mean my little Pommie?' she replied. 'As in a person from England. Not a potato from France.'

'Er, right, yeh, okay, right, whatever,' stuttered a slightly fazed Dylan and quickly changed the tack of the conversation. 'How did you enjoy the bungee jump? Good to see you didn't get dipped too far into the water and lose my number.'

'I was always confident that wasn't going to happen with a man of your ability in charge,' replied Katie, trying not to return the purr, but not making a great job of it.

'I always try to look after my special customers,' warbled Dylan.

Katie decided that all this billing and cooing needed to stop. She was starting to feel like a slightly salacious Squirrel Nutkin. There was an uncomfortable silence before Dylan seemed to come down to earth. He asked Katie where she was staying and rather formally asked if he could drive up the coast to meet her and share a couple of schooners together. Perhaps at the weekend if he wasn't too busy at the bungee jump.

'Okay, ring me back, tell me when you can make it and I'll see what I can do,' replied Katie, surprising herself with her high levels of self-confidence coupled with knavish impudence.

She bade her goodbyes, ended the call then tutted in frustration. She had forgotten to ask him his real name.

NINE

After breakfast the following day, Larry invited Katie into his hotel room for a touch of help on the information technology front.

He explained that he wanted to reply to a tweet put out there by a guy called Jamal Jawai, a personality in the rather popular world of Australian rugby league.

'Never heard of him,' said Katie.

'Neither have I,' replied her kid brother.

Larry proceeded to tell his sibling all about his strange television encounter with the Aboriginal guy and his big hair, relating the story of how elders in his village were confidently predicting that a rogue asteroid had strayed off its customary orbital course and was heading towards earth, bringing with it unimaginable death and destruction.

'So what?' asked Katie, trying to look at least half-interested because her mind was almost entirely distracted by thinking about what kind of car Dylan might drive.

An open-top sports car would be nice.

'This guy's prediction about this asteroid crashing into earth is exactly what Michael, my Skype friend in America, is telling me. Nobody's listening to him and nobody seems to be listening to this Australian chap either. Are you listening to me Katie?'

'Yeh, yeh, every word,' she replied unconvincingly. 'So, what do you want to do about the asterisk thing then?'

Perhaps he's got a vintage MG. Like Rigsby. Dad would chuckle at that.

Larry managed to maintain his composure. Just. 'Well, if I can contact this Jamal chap, I could tell him that he's not the only one who believes this asteroid strike is actually going to happen. Let's have it right, he'll probably ignore me. I suspect he's already had enough of being laughed at. Then again, he might be glad of the support from someone who actually thinks there's something in it even if it is only coming from an adolescent Pom on holiday with his mum and dad with a daft mate on the other side of the Atlantic.'

'How old do you reckon Dylan is?' murmured Katie.

'I knew you weren't listening,' snapped Larry. 'Just tell me how to get in touch with Jamal.'

▼

Jamal Jawai opened his Twitter account and scrolled down the many messages and replies.

Several still made references to his rogue asteroid theory, many disparaging, several insulting, the rest sceptical at best.

He scanned and quickly deleted them, shaking his head slowly and sadly as he did so. But as he scrolled down quicker and quicker, his eye caught just one word – "believe".

He cast his eyes back to the start and read the whole message. A young English boy called Larry, on holiday in Sydney, had watched the televised interview about Jamal's asteroid theory and had seen it in a completely different light. He believed Jamal could be right. A colleague, an amateur astronomer in America, was predicting the same collision with this misbehaving heavenly body and the teenager was insisting they both had faith in Jamal and his sage village elders even if nobody else did. Larry had asked Jamal if he could meet him to discuss their remarkably similar experiences and had left a mobile number. Jamal, emotions hovering somewhere between pleasant surprise and sceptical uncertainty, read all the words again and thought hard.

He was, if the truth be known, rather looking forward to seeing the back of sniggering media sniping about his imminent end of the world theory. Sam had drained every last chuckle out of it and Jamal was keenly anticipating his return to the killing rugby league fields of Sydney where life was just about as real and chuckle-free as it got.

Yet his faith in Jenny held strong. She would undoubtedly have seen the television interview that made him out to be a bit of a prat and thinking about this made him sad, not least because Jenny had stared up at the stars and told him of her prediction with such belief and sincerity. Jamal could handle Sam the court jester having a laugh at his mate and making good television at his expense, but could Jenny? He had long felt sorry for woman to whom he owed so much. He had long felt sorry for his own Aboriginal people to whom he owed so much. With a resolute punch of the desktop delivered by a truly massive fist, Jamal made up his mind.

He would contact the English kid.

TEN

Larry's mobile phone pinged and trilled and flashed up the arrival of a text from an unknown number.

Larry frowned and thought about deleting what was sure to be the rock-solid assurance that he had won pots of cash/ was due an immense PPI payment/was entitled to compensation after being deafened when he worked in a wasp factory back in the sixties/ had been anointed the new crown prince of East Timor.

But he still opened the text, read it, gasped, read it again, gasped again, and in a state of highly-charged animation kick-started Skype to talk to Michael with a matter of supreme urgency. He didn't care what time it was in Texas.

Michael's slightly pixelated face appeared on the screen and Larry immediately launched into a breathless, frenzied, and thoroughly exaggerated account of how one Jamal Jawai, Australia's most famous sporting celebrity and fabulous on-trend personality, had not only sent him a stunning text, but had suggested that they urgently meet up to talk about the imminent end of civilisation and what they, the 21st century caped crusaders, could do to save the doomed planet from the Invasion of the Killer Asteroid. He and Jamal were leading out the first team. Indiana Jones had been dropped to the substitutes' bench.

'And it's all down to you and your Dad', added Larry, wheezing and perspiring slightly.

'Wow!' hollered Michael. 'Go for it brother. I'll go tell my dad straight away. Even if it is two in the morning. He's going to be excited as we are. Wow! You have to keep in touch and tell me everything this guy says and what you're going to do next. I feel so helpless so many miles away. I so wish I could be with you. Right, I'm going to wake my Dad and I'm betting my bottom dollar we'll go straight up to the telescope to take another look at this bad ass asteroid dude. It's been two hours since we last looked. Speak to you soon Larry. Don't be a stranger.'

▼

Katie's mobile shrilled and she picked up the call a little more quickly than she had intended.

'Hi Dylan', she said. 'Before we go any further, I would like to ask you what your real name is.'

'Oh, right, did I actually mention that?' replied Dylan, slightly bemused and sounding genuinely surprised.

'Yeh, up there on the bungee jump. So, what is it?'

'Do you really have to know?'

'Yeh.'

'Promise you won't laugh.'

'Promise.'

'Prestige.'

'Prestige?!' snorted Katie, placing her hand on her mouth and unsuccessfully trying to stifle a hearty guffaw sneaking through the serried ranks of several closed fingers.

'You promised,' whined Prestige, wholly unimpressed. 'It was all my bloody dad's fault. He got well pissed on the night I was born and was so pleased he had a boy managed to lose the plot completely.'

'So how did you get from Prestige to Dylan?'

'The boys at the jump thought I looked like Bob Dylan used to look, you know, that hippie guitar guy from the seventies. It stuck…thankfully.'

'So, they felt sorry for you…is that what you mean?'

'Yeh. Whatever. What are you doing on Saturday night?'

'Meeting you. Be outside our hotel at half seven. I'll text you the address. Oh, and Prestige?'

'What?'

'Don't be late.'

▼

Jamal Jawai, feeling a tad sheepish, pulled his rather boastful large car to a halt in a swirl of dust outside Jenny's ramshackle home. Mellow shadows stretched lazily over a half-hearted grassy sward. Rooks wheeled. Jamal again leapt up the small flight of steps on to the creaking verandah in a single leap.

He was feeling surprisingly nervous. He knew that Jenny would have seen the rather surreal television interview with Sam the Man and felt he had a lot to explain. Jenny walked out on to the verandah, smiled warmly and greeted her beloved hero with the best hug she could muster, long on effort, but short on reach, her arms failing to meet either side of two monster shoulders blades.

She sat down, poured the teas, re-arranged the sticky buns on her makeshift tray and looked at Jamal, her eyes a blend of admonishment and admiration.

'Sam and his friends had a right old chuckle at our expense, didn't they?' she remarked.

Jamal noted the use of the word "our". This meant that Jenny must have taken the television ribaldry personally, and possibly seriously. Beneath the bright studio lights and before a braying audience, Jamal had endured dismay and disappointment in equal measure, but felt he had the self-esteem and character to overcome. Not to mention a thoroughly successful rugby league career. One swashbuckling try on his return to the NRL and all mention of killer asteroids would be immediately dispatched to the dustbin of media history. Jenny, however, could enjoy no such escape.

So, he decided to stay positive and tell Jenny all about their new fan club and how they ought to embrace the support of his new English friend and an obscure American amateur star-gazer.

'We do have friends who believe in us', he said to Jenny, reaching across the table and taking her hand. 'Friends from all over the world in fact.'

Jamal proceeded to relate the story about his rather unexpected encounter with Larry, the young boy from England and his co-conspirator from across the Atlantic, both of whom had much faith in his asteroid theory. Their asteroid theory, he hastened to add.

'What do you think we should do?' asked Jenny

'Larry's on holiday here in Sydney. I think we should invite him to our home, take him to the special place and show him the stars.'

'I think that's a wonderful idea Jamal. Have a sticky bun.'

ELEVEN

George and Gaynor faced the prospect of an evening in Sydney on their own. They were both rather looking forward to it. However, they had been rather taken aback when they learned of the twin trails of adventure along which their children were about to embark that same night.

Larry and Katie had both rocked up at their parents' room earlier in the evening and produced eye-popping tales of impending encounters with native Australians. Their daughter's date with dastardly Dylan from the bungee jump was possibly more of a gentle surprise than a shock. Mum and dad had noticed a simmering chemistry between the two high above the water, Dylan's rather inventive secretion of a slip of paper in a back pocket a source of some wry amusement to the members of the more mature generation.

But Larry's explanation for his absence was a far more complex and bewildering beast. George and Gaynor had been vaguely aware of their son's long-range American friend and his theory about a life-destroying asteroid, but had, like many others, been somewhat dismissive. Now Larry had told them all about his bizarre television encounter with a rugby league star and how "this leading sporting celeb" was going to meet him and explain why he too agreed that an asteroid was on a collision course with earth.

It was all a bit much for George and Gaynor to take on board, especially when both son and daughter insisted that mum and dad stay out of the way. Larry and Katie, by complete coincidence, were both being picked up outside the hotel at 7.30pm.

'We hardly know this Dylan and this Aboriginal man that you're meeting Larry is a total stranger,' griped Gaynor. 'How do we know you're going to be okay? Larry's only sixteen.'

'Oh, do stop fussing mother,' snapped Katie. 'We've both got our 'phones. I'll report in on the hour if you want.'

Gaynor glared at her daughter, but George came to the rescue with a plan, which, surprisingly, only met with token resistance. After the ironing out of a few quibbles, there was a collective nodding of heads. Larry and Katie both agreed to be back in the hotel bar at about 11.30pm where they would meet up with George and Gaynor. Then mum and dad would know all parties were safe and would get to meet the new strangers in their midst.

▼

Larry and Katie made their way down to the hotel lobby together. Both were feeling nervous, but there was also a hint of pending excitement in the air. On time, 7.30pm, they pushed open the main glass door, walked into the balmy early evening air and spotted two cars parked in the short stay pick-up bay. One of them was a sleek and shiny SUV, the other was a small, rusting wreck.

Katie suspected which was Dylan's. It wasn't an open top and it wasn't an MG. Ex-mechanic dad would have called it a nail. Or a shed.

Dylan clambered out of the fiasco on four wheels and thankfully looked marginally more presentable than his motor. His hair was neatly tied back, his open-neck shirt was clean and pressed, and his jeans had only one hole in them. He bustled over to Katie, who was standing next to her brother. Dylan recognised Larry from the bungee jump. Dylan started to speak but was distracted by big movement on his starboard side, spotting a large, well-dressed Aboriginal guy walking towards them. Dylan recognised him at once: Jamal Jawai, rising star of the NRL. Bit of a looker and a media darling. What in the name of Ned Kelly was he doing here?

Jamal slowed as he approached the gaggle of agog youngsters and hesitated briefly before Larry dug deep into his small reservoir of pluck and stepped forward to greet the new arrival with an outstretched hand. It disappeared from view.

'I'm Larry. You must be Jamal. So pleased to meet you mate.'

'Great to meet you Larry. You're a long way from home.'

They exchanged further pleasantries before Larry introduced his sister and then turned uncertainly to Dylan and dithered. He thought for a few seconds before describing him as a "family friend who's good with ropes."

Dylan wasn't listening anyway. He just stood open-mouthed and in total awe of the wholly surreal scenario unfolding before him. Why was this bloody Jamal Jawai guy here? The plot thickened considerably when Jamal placed a very large arm around Larry's shoulders, bade his farewells and the pair of them traipsed off towards the menacing SUV loitering with intent under the sun's last few rays of the day. The SUV blended a purr and a growl as it pulled out of the parking bay. Dylan's eyes followed the car every inch of the way before it was lost from view. He turned to Katie with a million questions to ask.

Katie sensed his bewilderment.

She grabbed his hand and started walking. 'Let's get in the car. I'll tell you all about it on the way to wherever we're going.'

The Fiasco started first time.

TWELVE

Jamal and Larry cruised through the outskirts of the city and quickly left the bustle behind.

Jamal was dressed in blue jeans, a stunningly white t-shirt and a denim jacket, sleeves rolled up to reveal a host of tattoos running up massively muscular forearms. He had even more hair than Dylan, most of it piled high on his head and held in captivity by a large black band. This was one extraordinarily big human being, but Larry didn't find him intimidating and liked his new friend almost instantly. Jamal spoke to the teenager on equal terms, treated him as a fellow adult, was candid, honest and interesting.

They discussed their differing encounters with trespassing heavenly bodies, the roles of various interested parties and shared a chortle at the televised antics of Sam the Man, even if he had been most dismissive of Jamal's fears. Fears that had brought them together. Larry listened attentively as Jamal outlined in some detail the role that his dear friend Jenny had played, not only in his life, but also in her convincing theory of a rogue asteroid and the destruction it may bring. He explained how she had gazed at the stars at one of the Aboriginal sacred sites and how his confidence in her remained intact despite a much-publicised encounter with mass indifference and collective cynicism.

'And if it's okay with you, I'm going to pick up Jenny then we can all visit the sacred site together.'

Jamal briefly took his eyes off the road and glanced across at Larry.

'That's just fine', Larry replied, meeting the eye contact.

'I wondered where we were going.'

▼

Jenny was ready and waiting on the dusty road outside her home.

Jamal helped her clamber into the back seat despite Larry's offer to let her sit in the front. Jenny explained that she preferred to remain anonymous in such an ostentatious car. Larry smiled weakly and nodded uncertainly. He wasn't too sure what ostentatious meant.

The SUV rode majestically over the deepening pot holes pitting the deteriorating roads which became rough-hewn tracks as they entered the outskirts of the outback. The fading light slowly obscured dry, coarse scrubland interspersed with dust-laden rattan palms and spreading eucalyptus trees shedding huge shards of bark.

Jamal drove on relentlessly and eventually pulled the vehicle to a halt near the sacred site by the river. The three of them made their way on foot to the edge of an oxbow lake, the relatively still waters formed by the sluggish meander of the river over countless years. Nature had generously provided a gentle, sandy beach with calm, lapping waters, yet there was no sea in sight.

The star-gazers settled on the soft sand and looked upwards to space. The night was clear and still and once more there was a host of heavenly objects demanding their attention.

'It's not the same again', whispered Jenny.' The pattern has changed.'

Larry looked at her in some bewilderment.

'I'll draw you a map,' she said.

Jenny asked to Jamal to smooth down a few feet of damp sand with his monster hands and pulled a broken pencil from her bag. In the sand she drew a rough and partial diagram of our solar system, Earth, Mars, Mercury and Venus in orbit around the sun, the main asteroid belt doing much the same, but deeper in space. Dragging her pencil across the sand, Jenny demonstrated how a rogue asteroid could escape this orbit and come hurtling towards Earth and other planets. 'This is what our ancient ancestors told of and there's no reason to believe that anything is different today,' she said, quietly.

Jamal nodded in agreement, rose to his feet and padded a few metres across the sand to the water's edge where he knelt to wash his hands. Larry looked up at the twinkling, light-laden heavens, but as he gazed in awe he was startled by a noise, the like of which he had never heard before. It was hard to define, an unnatural surge and sluck of water followed almost instantaneously by the rush of rapidly moving air right next to where Jamal was kneeling. Larry turned to the shore and witnessed a horrendous sight, a forbidding array of dripping white teeth rising from the shallows powered upwards by a large, dark grey, reptilian body.

Jenny screamed then Jamal screamed and hurled himself backwards, but the crocodile's open jaw snapped shut with a rapid, vicious bite which trapped Jamal's forearm. The crocodile twisted, its huge body providing immense traction, the thrust wrenching Jamal sideways and dragging him into the water. Blood spouted from his arm and the crocodile briefly released its grip only to thrust again and snap shut again, higher up his victim's arm.

Jamal's second scream was born of agony as his shoulder was pierced by lacerating, unforgiving teeth. Again, the crocodile twisted before launching itself backwards, dragging Jamal down into deeper water, the animal thrashing and turning as its flailing victim disappeared under the surface, a surface which seemed to boil red with blood. Jenny screamed again and ran to the edge of the water, but there was nothing she could do. The surface swirled and then stilled. The ultimate predator had its prey and was heading for the depths. Jenny stared out in horror over the now quiet waters. She cried out in anguish, dropped to her knees and beat the sand with her fists.

Larry had not moved, stunned into a fearful silence by the unreality of it all: a sixteen-year-old boy the prime witness to the gruesome and macabre death of a new friend he had met just a few hours earlier. And not just an ordinary punter. A professional athlete on his way to becoming a national sporting treasure.

Larry stared bleakly at Jenny, an ageing lady sitting forlornly in the sand, floods of tears pouring down a face etched with pure unhappiness. They were alone and stranded on the edge of nowhere he knew.

Larry felt he ought to say something to Jenny, offer consolation, compassion, but no words were forthcoming because his mind was blocked by the same thought coursing through it. He thought about how Jamal had suffered a horrible death because of him and his actions.

Suddenly, he felt very helpless and very much alone.

He needed help. They both needed help.

Larry pulled his mobile out of his pocket and lit the screen. Signal poor, very poor in fact. He rang his sister. It was switched off. He looked across the sand at Jenny and suddenly another terrible thought crossed his mind. The old lady was slouched and sobbing in the sand near the water's edge. Crocodile hunting ground.

Larry sprang to his feet, ran across the sand and half-led, half-dragged Jenny to safety. As he tried to re-assure her, inspiration struck.

'Jenny! What's the emergency phone number here in Australia?'

'What?'

'The emergency phone number… to speak to the police and rescue people. What is it?'

'Er…three zeros', whimpered Jenny. 'Yes, that's right, I think…I can't really think straight.'

Larry hit the buttons and an operator answered at once.

'I need the police, rescue and ambulance,' barked Larry, immediately wondering if he really needed all three.

'What's up mate?' replied Corey in a concerned, but still affable Australian accent.

'I was by this river and an Aboriginal guy's been killed by a crocodile. It came right out of the water. He didn't stand a chance.'

"Another bloody Abbo scoffed by a croc," thought a cynical Corey, but quickly moved on.

'Where are you mate?'

'Not a clue…somewhere in or near the Outback. I'm English, here on holiday. Completely lost. I'm with another woman. An Aboriginal woman.'

'What about this guy killed by a croc? Was he with you?'

'Yes, he was, you might know him,' said Larry. 'He's called Jamal Jawai. I believe he's big in rugby league.'

'Jamal Jawai!? The Sydney Barracudas' centre? He's the guy that's been scoffed by the croc?!' exclaimed Corey. 'Jeez, you can't be serious.'

'Yes, that's him. Now are you going to help us?'

'Too bloody true we are. Don't worry about being lost. I can track the position of your phone on the satellite. This is a full-on, all-stations alert and we'll be with you before you can say Mal Meninga. Stay where you are and stay on the line for as long as you can. We're coming in.'

"Jamal Jawai scoffed by a croc. Jeez…what a night this is going to be," thought Corey.

An anonymous Aboriginal man taken by a crocodile, strolling, presumably drunk, next to a lazy river in a backwater with no name would ordinarily attract little more official police attention than a delayed and cursory visit by a patrol car once it had filled its quota of speeding fines.

But the shock killing of golden boy Jamal Jawai was a whole different ball game.

An animated Corey was busy calling out everybody. He was considering calling out the military. He was certainly calling out his mate in the press.

THIRTEEN

J enny and Larry sat on the sand and waited. The moon offered a modicum of comforting light, but not enough to lift the gloom of the dark mood after the terrible events that had just unfolded before them.

Conversation was sparse and difficult, and time trickled by.

After what seemed like an eternity, a pair of headlamps came bumping down the nearby track and a vehicle pulled to a jerking halt behind Jamal's SUV. Relief coursed through Larry's every pore.

'Stay where you are…I can see you,' cried an urgent voice as hurried, running steps made their way down to the river, the path ahead inadequately illuminated by the light from a mobile phone. A late to middle-aged man gasping for breath stopped by their side. He was wearing suede shoes, a pair of lightly-coloured slacks, an open-necked shirt and a casual beige jacket. A half-smoked cigarette nestled in one hand, a small digital recorder in the other. He started to speak, initially rather uncertainly. 'Er...are you the guys who called the emergency services?'

'Yeh,' replied Larry, wondering exactly which emergency service their new friend represented. He looked like he'd just rushed out of the pub. He had just rushed out of the pub.

'So, you're the guys who were with Jamal Jawai?'

'Yeh,' repeated Larry, looking the newcomer up and down and casting him a puzzled stare.

'Hi. I'm Phil Reynolds from the Sydney Bugle. Is it right that Jamal's been scoffed by a bloody croc?'

Before a stunned Larry had time to answer or even ask how a newspaper reporter had got there before the emergency teams, the air began to fill with noise, thwack, thwack, thwack, followed by the bright beam of a powerful searchlight. A helicopter was bearing down on them. Then there were blaring sirens and more blazing headlights on the road at the top of the beach, dust flying and beefy tyres crunching as what seemed like a convoy of speeding vehicles arrived at the scene.

There were more shouts, more hurried steps and now bright torch lights as policemen, rescue teams and medics descended on Larry and Jenny. An indignant Phil Reynolds was trying to elbow his way back to the front to get an answer to the only question he was interested in. A policeman and a senior medic glared at him and told him to shove off. The policeman called for calm and knelt beside a sobbing Jenny. He took her hand. 'Are you okay?' he asked gently. 'It looks like you've both been through quite an ordeal.'

Jenny nodded weakly. 'It's been truly awful. We're not hurt, but Jamal...'

The medic said, 'We have reports that somebody's been taken by a crocodile. Is this true?'

Jenny nodded, pointed to the water and wailed, 'Just over there by the river. My own Jamal...my poor Jamal.'

'You mean Jamal Jawai the rugby league player? The rumour's true then?'

'Yes,' Jenny sobbed, 'There's nothing you can do. He's dead.'

'We'll still organise a search just in case. Tell us more about what's happened.'

Jenny and Larry related the story of the night, the circumstances that had brought the three of them together, the reason they had visited the sacred site and the terrible turn of fate that had befallen them.

The two men listened attentively and nodded sympathetically throughout, the policeman then rising to his feet.

'First of all, I'll need some contact details from you both, then I'll take you home. We'll probably need to talk to you both again, but that can all wait until tomorrow. I think you've both been through enough for one night. And we need to get you away from the hyenas pretty pronto.'

'The hyenas?' asked Larry. 'They've not got those in Australia as well as crocodiles, have they?'

'The leader of the pack's here already. I'm talking about the press.'

The policeman led Larry and Jenny to his car. Phil Reynolds narrowed his eyes and watched them all the way as he jabbered excitedly into his mobile phone.

FOURTEEN

Larry settled in the back of the police vehicle and pulled out his phone.

In the front, the inspector was calling friends and relatives on behalf of Jenny to ensure she had comfort and support when she was dropped off first. Larry again tried to ring his sister, but still to no avail. Desperate times called for desperate measures. He was going to have to call his mum. Mum picked up straight away. She sensed something was wrong straight away. How wrong things really were she soon discovered as Larry delivered the shocking events of the night, chapter and verse.

'Oh, my days Larry, I can't believe this has happened. Where are you now?'

'On my way back to the hotel in the back of a police car. I should be in time to meet you at half eleven. I've tried to tell Katie, but she's not picking up.'

'I'll try her,' gasped Gaynor. 'But now I have to go. Your dad's desperate to know what's going on and should know. We'll see you soon.'

Gaynor turned to George, her face pale with more than a hint of ashen. She chose her words carefully. 'First of all, that was Larry ringing from the back of a police car. But don't worry, he's not in trouble or injured. He's fine. He's on his way back here.'

She drew a deeper breath. 'But that Jamal guy, the rugby player that Larry met…he's dead. They went to a river and he's been attacked by a crocodile. Oh, my dear God George, I can't believe this has happened.'

George couldn't believe it either. He slumped heavily back on to his sofa in the down town Sydney pub that had been their choice of night out. They ditched their drinks on the table and headed back to the hotel.

▼

Katie and Dylan walked into the hotel bar shortly before eleven o'clock after a rather successful and enjoyable night out together, much of the evening taken up by Katie's explanation of why superstar Jamal Jawai had turned up, the surreal events leading up to the meeting and where and why he and Larry had gone.

They were early at the hotel to meet Katie's parents – as requested – not least because Dylan faced a long drive home and needed to be out of bed early in the morning to "work with ropes."

Gaynor and George were nowhere to be seen. Katie reached for and then switched on her phone. She had turned if off to stop her mother nagging during fun time with a date. She started to push buttons.

Dylan was distracted by the television on the wall and the start of the late-night news. He looked on with some interest at dramatic floodlit footage of a hovering helicopter directing a powerful search light on to dark, forbidding waters. Numerous rescue vehicles with flashing orange lights were parked haphazardly by the side of a slow-flowing river. There were close-up shots of footprints in soft sand. Then the camera zoomed in on face of a reporter live at the scene, the hack grimly announcing the shock-horror death of Sydney Barracudas' rugby league centre Jamal Jawai, the star sportsman believed to have been savagely torn to pieces by a monster crocodile deep in the bad lands of the bleak, barren Outback.

Hyperbole had already set in.

The reporter sought further gravitas before announcing that, although the search was continuing, there was little hope of finding Jamal alive. But there was strong speculation that the victim had not been not alone when he had been dragged to his watery grave alongside the river of death.

'The question,' he asked, leaning forward and looking menacing, 'is this. Who was Jamal with and what were they doing in this dangerous, desolate place, miles from civilisation?'

This was technically two questions, but the whole of Australia still needed to know.

Dylan listened intently and stared at the screen in stunned silence. He turned from the television and virtually ordered Katie to get off her phone.

'Did you see the news? That Jamal Jawai guy, the rugby player out with your brother tonight...he's dead!' Dylan exclaimed.

'Dead? No, he can't be. You're wrong.'

Katie's phone trilled and instinct told her to answer it, even though it was her mum. Her face filled with horror as a sobbing Gaynor confirmed Dylan's shocking revelation.

'It's the lead story on the late-night television news Mum, helicopters, flashing lights, live coverage,' Katie gasped.

'You're joking! Listen, we're only five minutes from the hotel,' replied Gaynor. 'We'll meet you in the bar. Get me a brandy. A big one.'

▼

The only drink on the table in the hotel bar was Gaynor's double brandy and that remained untouched.

The five people sitting around it were in need of a reality check. Larry had related the surreal saga of the night – and then repeated it in even greater detail – and his words still seemed like an unwanted stranger in the room, words that were way beyond the realm of the small, unassuming world usually inhabited by the Longworths.

George was stunned – he felt the overwhelming urge to speak to Bernard – but had to make do with Dylan. The teenager, however, was making a lot of sense. The young man, despite feeling slightly overwhelmed, pointed out that Larry, and indeed the rest of his family, were about to become hot property. They would surely be pursued by the many branches of the media who would want to know why Jamal was with Larry – and Jenny for that matter –

and exactly what they had been doing by the river when an Australian hero had been killed.

'They're not going to give up. Jamal's a big name in a big sport and they will want a lot of answers to a lot of questions,' warned Dylan. 'I can well imagine that the television people will want to get involved as well.'

Larry nodded in agreement. He privately recalled Jamal's television appearance and was immediately reminded of the reason he had met his new Australian friend…to talk about their mutual belief in the imminent arrival of a killer asteroid. Yet again, responsibility for Jamal's death weighed heavily on Larry's young shoulders.

Now it seemed certain that he would not only have to speak to the police again, but also a drooling press. Or the rabid hyenas as they were known locally. He would have to explain the asteroid theory he shared with Jamal, the same theory that had provided the source of such hilarity and ridicule for Sam the Man and his many mates in front of a chuckling nation. It was all too much for Larry's saturated brain to take on board.

The teenager was jerked out his reverie by rapid movement to his left. Gaynor lunged forward, grabbed her double brandy and lashed it down in one.

'I think we all need to go to bed. I suspect it's going to be a long day tomorrow. And you need to go home Dylan. Sorry to have dragged you into all this.'

'No need to apologise Mrs L', Dylan replied, clambering to his feet. 'It's been one of the most interesting nights out I've had in a long time.'

Dylan nodded to Katie and they headed for the exit. Larry and his parents walked over to the lift.

George took Gaynor's hand.

'Well love, you said all along it was going to be the unforgettable holiday of a lifetime,' he volunteered as two silver metal doors slid apart.

'On track so far.'

▼

Phil Reynolds had slipped into full gloat mode. There was much evidence of smugness too.

The Sydney Bugle's front page – and several pages inside – were given over in their entirety to the ghastly death of Jamal Jawai.

Under a large banner headline and rather distasteful picture by-line on the front, Reynolds exclusively and breathlessly revealed that he had been the first person on the scene after Jamal had suffered a gruesome and bloody death. The sporting hero had been alongside a desolate river with a teenage boy and an elderly woman when one of Australia's national treasures had died in the jaws of a monster. It was thought that the teenager was English, the elderly lady an Aboriginal, possibly from the nearby village of Jamal's birth.

The hack also proudly revealed that he had been the first newsman on the story following a hot tip from "a reliable source close to the rescue services." Readers were assured that the search for the identities of the mystery pair who were with Jamal was now underway. The page also carried three large pictures of Jamal, two of the rescue units near the river of death and one of a very large, very angry-looking crocodile with lots of vicious teeth, though possibly not the culprit.

FIFTEEN

Larry awoke early.

He had slept surprisingly well, despite the outrageous events of the previous night, all of which came pouring into his thoughts as soon as his eyes opened. It was all quite unreal and as he wondered what he ought to be doing next, the decision was taken for him. His mobile rang. It was the police. The desk sergeant was polite and non-threatening. He asked Larry if they could possibly see him later that day. He could bring his mum and dad if he wanted to. In fact, they ought to come because he was only sixteen. And because they were strangers in a strange land and had become embroiled in such a gruesome incident, a car would pick them up at their hotel.

Larry replied with all the right words, went to tell his mum and dad and the rendezvous was arranged. Katie was to attend too.

▼

The Longworth family were handed hot cups of coffee and escorted to an interview room deep in the heart of the police station by a junior female officer.

On the business side of the desk were sitting a uniformed officer and a plain-clothes detective. On the visitors' side were five chairs, one already occupied by Jenny who smiled vaguely at the new arrivals beneath sad, tear-filled eyes. The policemen stood up and shook hands with the Longworths. The detective introduced himself as DC Brandon Carter, his uniformed colleague, he informed them, was PC Jonathan Mort. Larry recognised him as the policeman he had spoken to next to the river shortly after Jamal had been killed. DC Carter asked Larry and Jenny to sit next to each other and then asked them to re-live the events prior to and leading up to the fateful night. This they duly did, from their meeting in the village, their journey to the river and the reasons they were there. Jenny described how they had gazed at the stars in the heavens before Jamal flattened the damp sand for her map and then left them to wash his hands in the shallow water only to encounter his gruesome death.

'I believe you were gazing at the stars looking for an asteroid which is heading to earth', said PC Mort.

Jenny nodded and looked even more morose.

DC Carter made some reassuring noises before telling the family they weren't being interviewed in connection with an illegal act. They were not under suspicion, the police had just wanted the story of the night in their own words, particularly from Larry and Jenny, the eye witnesses.

Now PC Mort had something to tell them. He turned to his colleague and handed him the stage. PC Mort looked a tad nervous and glanced anxiously over at Jenny before speaking.

'Er, Larry…can I ask you a question first?'

Larry nodded.

'What was Jamal wearing when you first met him?'

Larry thought for a few seconds before replying, 'Jeans, a white t-shirt and a denim jacket.'

'And did Jamal have tattoos on his arms?'

'Lots.'

PC Mort also nodded before explaining that the rescue teams had spent many hours searching the river, just in case. There was no miracle rescue to report, but they were able to confirm that Jamal had been killed by a crocodile. They were, at least, as certain as they could be.

'There's been no body recovered, but one of the rescue boats found a recently severed arm washed up on a sandbank on the other side of the river. It was tattooed, and the remains of a denim jacket were still attached to it.'

Jenny burst into tears. PC Mort handed her a tissue and floundered before re-gaining his composure.

He continued, 'Sorry to have to tell you such a gruesome detail, but every possibility has to be eliminated from our inquiries and if we can satisfy the coroner that a crocodile attack was the accidental cause of death then we can hopefully avoid any more interviews, formalities and further upset.'

Jenny looked a million miles from reassured while Larry looked toward mum and dad for support. PC Mort's words had soared right over his muddled head. DC Carter wrested control. 'We'll need written statements from you all, but a bit later perhaps, and we have officers who will help you with those. In the meantime, you're all free to carry on with your normal lives.'

It was DC Carter's turn to hesitate before he carried on speaking.

'However, normality may not return too quickly. I don't know how aware you are of exactly who Jamal is, or should I say, was. He was a very well-known sporting personality in this country and you all know how seriously we Australians take our sport, especially rugby league, our national obsession. He was also quite an out-going personality, very popular on television. I believe young Larry here saw him on one of those sporting celebrity programmes.'

Larry nodded. He was doing a lot of nodding.

DC Carter continued, 'What I'm trying to say is this. Jamal's death is going to be a big story. Already is in fact. The press are going to want to know all the gruesome details and they're not going to give up easily. How much you co-operate with them is up to you, but once they've got their teeth into something, they don't let go.'

The detective paused for a few seconds to reflect on his rather unfortunate choice of words but decided to move on quickly in the hope that he got away with it.

'The police can offer all manner of protection, but I'm afraid we'll struggle to keep the hyenas off your backs. What they do might offend a lot of people, but what they do isn't illegal.'

Hyenas. That word again thought Larry as he and his family and the two policemen made their way towards the exit and their awaiting lift back to the hotel. They pushed their way through the last glass door on to the paved area outside. A man slid out from behind a tile-clad post and sidled over to Larry. Larry recognised him immediately as the hyena from the beach, the newspaper journalist, the first person he had seen after Jamal's death.

'You must be Larry,' slavered Phil Reynolds, one hand on the trigger of his voice recorder. 'How ya feeling after ya best mate got scoffed by a croc?'

Before Larry had time to answer, DC Carter intervened with stern words. 'Why don't you bugger off Reynolds. I've warned you before about hanging about outside the police station like some bloody vulture. Sling your hook or I'll charge you with intimidating a witness.'

Reynolds glared at him, but still retreated. But as he did so, a photographer suddenly appeared from behind another post, pulled up a camera from his waist and fired off several rapid shots of the Longworths standing in a group outside the police station. He and Reynolds then fled.

'That's tomorrow's front page sorted,' mumbled DC Carter to no-one in particular. 'Come on let's take you home.'

▼

The police car pulled up outside their hotel. Larry got out first and noticed a man mountain standing next to the "A" frame advertising hoarding on the forecourt. He did a double-take. It was the same large, wild-haired Aboriginal person who was on the advert for the NRL game. It was Sam the Man standing next to a picture of himself.

On the framed photograph, Sam Runceman was grinning and carefree. In real life he was a picture of

143

misery. Larry took a few tentative steps towards him and as he did so, noticed something else. Tears were cascading down the big man's mournful face. Sam walked towards Larry and spoke his name out loud, although it was more of a lament than a greeting. The huge Aboriginal took the teenager in his arms, lifted him off his feet and embraced him with an all-enveloping hug. Larry tried to do much the same, but his arms wouldn't reach all the way around Sam's back, not least because it was about the same size as a single bed.

Larry started crying too. He didn't really know why.

Sam lowered Larry back on to his feet, placed his hands on the young man's shoulders and started to speak, weeping and wailing at the same time. 'My dear, dear English friend. You were the last person to see my beloved Jamal alive. That young man meant so much to me and now he's gone. My blood brother is lost. How can I ever forgive myself for what I've done?'

George and Gaynor looked on in amazement as the latest episode in this remarkable Australian soap opera of their own unfolded before their unbelieving eyes. Sam wiped his saturated cheeks with the back of his hand.

'Who on earth is that huge bloke hugging our Larry?' asked George.

'I wouldn't have a clue,' replied Gaynor. 'Perhaps we'd better go and find out.'

They walked over to their son who was still holding court with yet another mystery personality to breeze into the Longworths' roller-coaster adventure. Larry said, 'Sam, this is my mum and dad and my sister Katie. Family, this is Sam Runceman, otherwise known as Sam the Man.' Larry waved an arm in the vague direction of the "A" frame as if this was the only further explanation needed.

Sam shook hands with the rest of Larry's family and hugged them too. The tears continued to flow.

'Perhaps we should all go inside, have a drink and then somebody can tell Dad and I exactly what's going on,' suggested Gaynor.

'That's the best idea I've heard all day,' responded George and headed at a rate of knots towards the entrance door.

▼

Perched at the bar with his family and new friend, Larry explained how he had seen Sam the Man on television when they had first arrived in Australia.

Jamal had been one of the studio guests and Larry told how Sam had revealed Jamal's asteroid theory live in front of a studio audience. He hesitated before adding that Sam had picked up plenty of cheap laughs at Jamal's expense when he had poked fun at his pal's prediction that they were all going to die. Sam looked even more forlorn.

'His theory was the one I told you about dad,' added Larry. 'The one my American friend Michael Berlingo revealed on Skype…that a rogue asteroid is on a collision course with earth. Jenny saw it in the stars above her ancestors' sacred site and she believed it too.'

'Who's Michael Berlingo and who's Jenny?' asked a bewildered Sam the Man.

Larry explained who Michael and his father the amateur astronomer were before adding, 'Jenny was one of Jamal's village elders. Jamal seemed very close to her. I think she brought him up, helped to turn him into a great sportsman. She was with me when Jamal died,' replied Larry.

Sam placed his slowly shaking head in his hands before looking up with a look of even deeper anguish on his face.

'I feel so guilty about all of this. I feel so responsible for the death of one of my best friends and now the suffering that poor Jenny must be going through. If only I hadn't belittled him like that on television, none of this would have happened.'

'I feel guilty too,' whispered Larry. 'If only I hadn't got in touch with him.'

'Nobody's to blame,' interrupted Gaynor, a stern authority in her tone. 'Jamal's death was an accident, a complete accident. We wouldn't even be in this country if it wasn't for your father's illness…so is he to blame?'

Silence descended. George plucked pieces out of his beer mat and looked sheepish. Sam sensed he had trespassed into a family secret so steered the conversation in a different direction. He drew a deep breath and said,' I want to make it up to Jamal and I would like you all to help me.'

Four interested faces focused on Sam's craggy features.

'We should all go back on television, on to the same sports magazine programme and tell the Aussie nation about Jamal's asteroid theory without turning him into a laughing stock. We can explain the background, why he was by the river with Jenny and his young English friend and how he came to die.' Sam's voice faltered and cracked as he was reminded of his friend's death.

'We've been warned off dealing with the press and media,' said Larry. 'There's some reporter called Phil Reynolds who's on our case already. He was waiting outside the police station earlier today and they snatched some photographs of us all before the police told him to clear off. The police say he's a hyena.'

'I know all about that Reynolds and the way he operates,' snarled Sam. 'You'll get no sympathy out of that lot, but we're not like them, we're on your side. We're all in this together for the sake of Jamal.'

'So, we all get to appear on national television?' asked Katie, running her fingers through her hair and smoothing her jeans. Larry was also thinking that a spot of stardom was something he might enjoy.

Sam replied, 'I was certainly hoping that Larry would agree, and I was going to track down Jenny too because they were both with Jamal by the river. But why not mum and dad and sister too? You're all part of the story and I think it's an important story that needs to be told. Everybody involved should have their say, so are you all up for it?'

Gaynor looked at George who gave his wife a look which suggested he was resigned to his fate.

'We need to sleep on it, Sam', responded Gaynor, 'but perhaps we should do this. If we give the interviews and the whole story to you, then perhaps this Reynolds chap and his pet monkey will stop following us around and leaping out at us from behind posts.'

Sam smiled for the first time that day and declared, 'Let's do this for Jamal.'

SIXTEEN

It was late evening back at the hotel and George barged into Larry's room.

'Right techno kid. I want to speak to my neighbour Harry back home. Before we left, he told me that his wife Esme has got that Skype gizmo on her computer and that I could contact him using that. I need you to do this for me.'

Larry only moaned a bit before dragging his laptop across the bed. He pressed all the right buttons and a rather jumpy picture of Esme appeared on the screen. George moved close in to speak to her.

'Hi Esme. How's things? How's Bernard?'

'Bernard's fine, everything's fine. Is your holiday everything you expected it to be?'

'Yes, and quite a lot more', replied George.

'I'll go and get Harry for you.'

'Okay, but can I speak to Bernard first?'

'You want to speak to Bernard?'

'Yes.'

Esme failed to disguise her vague amusement, but left the room, returned a few minutes later and unceremoniously pulled the dog in front of the screen. Bernard gave a small whelp of pleasure when he saw his master. George would have whelped too had he been able to.

'Bernard, my old mate, great to see you. Food okay? Plenty of walks? Missing me? Yeh, missing you too. Now pay attention and listen to this lot.'

George proceeded to tell his dog the surreal story of their Australian adventure so far. The whole nine yards. Bernard listened attentively, the narrator more than convinced that his best mate was taking every word on board.

'… and now this Sam the Man character want us all to be interviewed on national television so that Larry and Jenny can explain exactly what happened on the night this Jamal chap was attacked by a bloody crocodile. What do you reckon to that Bernard? Is this something you think we should do?'

Bernard slowly laid down his head and lifted his right paw.

'That's a weight off my shoulders,' sighed George.

'We'll do it.'

'Cheers Bernard.'

▼

Larry also spent time on Skype that night but preferred the company of another human rather than a dog, Michael Berlingo in Texas.

He too passed on the full details of the saga so far, his American friend indulging in several sharp in-takes of breath as the stunning chapters were laid bare. He whistled long and loud when Larry told him of his impending television appearance, celebrity status looming.

'You know what this means. My dad's asteroid theory's going to get a public airing in front of an entire nation. I can't wait to tell him. This is fantastic news. Just so fantastic. What's the programme called and when's it on? I'm going to try and pick it up on the internet.'

'Don't know yet, but I'll let you know. I'm going to be so nervous,' replied Larry.

'You're nervous!' exclaimed Michael. 'Dad's not slept for days. He's been living in the attic gazing at the stars twenty-four seven and he's still smiling. I'm smiling too mate. Speak to you soon. Don't be a stranger just because you're nearly famous.'

▼

Katie was also dispensing the news that night, on her mobile phone telling Dylan all about her imminent star appearance on national television.

He, in return, told how the very public revelations of Jamal's gruesome death – and his puzzling connection with a mysterious English family – was all over news outlets like a cheap suit, newspapers, radio, television, the internet and social media alive with the macabre yet wholly absorbing story surrounding the premature end of such a young, yet still splendid sporting life.

Katie sensed that Dylan was a tad jealous of her involvement in this burgeoning media circus and she was nearly right. Dylan was, in fact, very jealous.

She said, 'I just don't know what I'm going to wear. I definitely need something new and I have to get my hair done.'

'Will you be okay on your own?' asked Dylan.

'I won't be on my own. I'll be surrounded by my family.'

'Oh, yeh. You're so lucky. To appear on television with Sam the Man. That's just bloody great. You've only been in the country five minutes and you're all going to be celebrities.'

'We're there to explain why this poor Jamal died,' replied Katie quietly. 'It's quite serious. I don't think Jenny will think it's bloody great.'

'Yeh, sorry, insensitive of me.'

An awkward silence was broken by Katie who decided it was time to stop tormenting her boyfriend. She knew Dylan was going to love her next suggestion.

'Sam the Man told us that he wanted everybody involved on that fateful night to appear on his show. I was nowhere near the river when Jamal died, but I'm still going to be a part of the programme. Do you want me to ask him if you can be on it too?'

'Aw, would you honey? That would be bloo…er, most considerate', blustered Dylan.

'How can I ever thank you?'

'You can find me a decent hairdresser and if you behave yourself, I might even not tell Sam that your real name is Prestige.'

▼

George and Gaynor lay side by side on top of their large hotel bed, handsomely propped up by more pillows than provided comfort for four sleepy heads in all three of their bedrooms back home.

They had just been told on the 'phone by a flustered receptionist that every other call coming into the hotel was from a newspaper, television or radio station wanting to speak to them. George had none-too-politely asked her if she minded telling them all to bugger off. The girl had said it would be a pleasure.

Now George and his wife were holding hands.

Gaynor tentatively asked her husband how he was coping with the enemy within.

'I've been too busy occupied with all the stuff that's going on over here to think about it much,' gushed George. 'Coping with cancer is a breeze compared to this lot. The entire population of the southern hemisphere wants to know who we are and what we're doing here. I knew we should have booked a caravan in Skegness.'

Gaynor smiled, leaned over and kissed George on the cheek. She was aware that this was his way of dealing with his illness. Deflect the focus elsewhere, inject a smidgeon of distracting, gentle humour. His way of coping. Perhaps the best way.

'We're all going to be appearing live on national television George. How on earth did that happen? We came here for a rest and a sun tan and now we're being pursued by a pack of baying hyenas, circling vultures, a large Aboriginal man called Sam and God knows how many more predatory wild beasts. Before we came over here, I read somewhere that Australia contains more poisonous, dangerous creatures than any other continent on earth. And that didn't even include the press.'

George laughed and gripped Gaynor's hand a bit tighter.

SEVENTEEN

At the National Aeronautics and Space Administration agency in Washington D.C., Professor David Emmerson finished speaking and put down the telephone.

A patient and studious man – essential attributes when working with the mind-boggling extremes of time and distance associated with outer space – meant that he had been willing to put aside a small amount of his precious time to hold another conversation with Maurice Berlingo, the amateur star-gazer who was once again of the firm opinion that a rogue asteroid was on course to collide with earth. The part-time astronomer had also excitedly reported the news that at least one sage Aboriginal in Australia was of the same opinion and would be airing her views on national television when she appeared on a sports magazine programme that also dealt with all matters rugby league.

Professor Emmerson kneaded a furrowed brow. He was more than slightly bemused by these latest revelations but kept his thoughts to himself. Rugby league? What on earth was that? However, he did recall checking the computer co-ordinates that the slightly hectoring Maurice Berlingo had provided the last time he'd made contact, his own software confirming the previous sighting of a potentially rogue celestial body on the prowl in this particular section of deep space. He had later re-run the co-ordinates through the computer and once again there were signs of unusual activity in the heavens, activity which strayed beyond the predictable and into the realm of 'better take a look at this.'

Professor Emmerson picked up the phone and asked to be put through to a higher authority, both literally and figuratively. The twin telescopes perched near the summit of Mount Mauna Kea on Hawaii were among the biggest and most powerful in the world.

Perhaps they ought to take a look.

EIGHTEEN

S am the Man had been a busy little bee. Well, a rather big busy bee actually.

After biding his time to let the family sleep on his request to reveal all on national television, Sam had assumed the green light was shining brightly and taken to the telephone with a vengeance.

He had spoken to Gaynor, George, Katie and Larry and with a little help from the latter had tracked down Jenny. They had all agreed to appear on the show together along with the usual panel of sporting cognoscenti and aspiring celebs. Katie had asked if her boyfriend – a hippie called Dylan, sometimes reluctantly also known as Prestige – could also appear. Sam, despite some bafflement, had shrugged his shoulders and brought to mind his earlier words...everybody involved should have their say.

He had then rather proudly informed his employers at the television station of his major scoop, first and exclusive interviews with the two people who were with Jamal by the river when he died along with the mystery English family and their intriguing involvement in this tragic, yet terrific tale.

Sam, however, was genuinely anxious to point out that he was not seeking to cover himself with journalistic glory. There would be no gloating. He simply wanted to make his peace with his lost friend, to make amends for the scorn he had poured on his asteroid theory, but most of all, to say sorry. This he had made clear to directors, producers, anchor men, cameramen, sound technicians and meal-time delivery men. In return, they would all be part of a storming television show featuring the amazing Longworth family, an Aboriginal elder called Jenny who had helped turn juvenile Jamal into a sporting hero and a long-haired hippie called Prestige. Although this was his real name, it wasn't to be mentioned. He now apparently, preferred to be called Dylan, which, in Sam's highly-regarded opinion, was possibly worse than Prestige.

Sam put down the phone for the last time and sighed deeply. It was a day's work well done. Public interest was already soaring and once the plugs and adverts had added to the clamour, Sam felt confident that the final television audience would smash the ratings.

The best show of his life so far was sorted.

▼

The boys in charge of the TV studio scenery had made an admirable effort in readiness for the programme of the decade.

Large photos of Jamal Jawai adorned the walls. There were splendid action shots featuring the player's immensely powerful frame, huge sculpted thighs, shoulders a metre across, rippling arm muscles. There were shots of him looking particularly gorgeous as he posed for the camera in his preferred casuals – denim jacket and glistening white t-shirt – leaning, albeit rather uncertainly, over the bonnet of his sponsored, ostentatious car. There was a shot of Jamal surfing with team mates, fellow NRL stars in gales of laughter as Jamal tumbled clumsily off his board into foaming white water.

On the backdrop behind the desk to be occupied by several studio experts was an array of large photos showing Jamal growing up. Sam had visited Jenny, Jamal's sage and mentor, and she had embraced his request for pictures of her protégé taken during his formative years.

Even when he was only eight years old, Jamal towered above nearly all the other youngsters in his village. Here they were remembered as a motley bunch, grinning inanely at the camera and laying collective hands on a cracked, worn and half-inflated old leather rugby ball. Their only ball. Despite the cheerful grins of the gathered kids and the presence of wholesome camaraderie, the dust and poverty from which Jamal had emerged was apparent. Even though there were youthful, seemingly carefree smiles, the blown-up images of an adolescent Jamal made for a solemn montage.

But then again, it was going to be a solemn evening.

▼

Sam the Man greeted Jenny, the Longworths and Dylan as his invited guests shuffled nervously into a cheerful studio

157

hospitality room a couple of hours before the live early evening broadcast.

Sam, a convivial and capable host, made all the introductions and tried to quell nerves. He explained what the programme wanted to achieve through interviews and via the medium of his guests' own descriptions; the background to the Longworth's trip to Australia; how they made contact with Jamal; the subsequent trip to the river and finally the asteroid theory, the main reason that was tying them all together.

Gaynor looked at George and George looked at Gaynor. The asteroid theory had undoubtedly played a lead role in the adventure so far, but it was far from the reason the family had flown to Australia.

Gaynor made a swift decision. She turned to Sam and Jenny and asked them if just the members of her family may have a few minutes on their own. They both gave understanding nods and stood up. Gaynor's one telling look at Dylan was all it took. The teenager nodded his comprehension and joined Sam and Jenny in upright mode before the three of them walked out of the room. The kid was more perceptive than perhaps Gaynor had given him credit for.

Once alone with her kith and kin, mother chaired the family meeting.

'The only reason we came over here to this country, as we all know, is your Dad's cancer,' Gaynor said, straight to the point. 'Now Sam has told us he wants the whole story. So, the question is, do we tell him about Dad?'

There was an uncomfortable silence, a silence perhaps surprisingly broken by Larry.

'The question is, do we tell him and a television audience reaching into the millions as well? This show is all over social media already you know. It's massive. Other sources are bound to pick it up. Tell Sam and we tell everybody. The pack of hyenas, the circling vultures and that lone wolf called Reynolds, they'll all be drooling and picking at our carcasses.'

George nodded in agreement and glanced in admiration at his son. Larry seemed to have matured three years in about the last three days. He wasn't sure a vulture drooled though.

'The decision has to be mine,' said George, placing his head in his hands. He quickly lifted his head.

'And I say we don't tell Sam the whole nine yards, perhaps just eight. Let's tell him that I've not been feeling too well, a dose of bad nerves with all this lot going on and leave it at that. I really can't be doing with all the fuss the whole truth will bring.'

The family murmured in agreement. Decision taken. Katie walked over to and opened the door and beckoned Sam, Jenny and Dylan back in. Gaynor explained to them that George wasn't feeling too great and this was why they had asked for a small family conference, just to make sure he wanted to go ahead with a live television interview and all the stress that would involve. Sympathy and understanding abounded. Sam assured them he would be tact and diplomacy personified.

Collectively, the guests made their way to make-up, following the signs affixed to seemingly endless corridors laden with garish photo shots of completely unfamiliar Australian celebrities. Gaynor knew that George would refuse all cosmetics. If Bernard had said it was alright though, she mused, her husband would probably would have gone before the cameras wearing more foundation than a Kardashian.

As the party walked along, Dylan trailed and dawdled several yards behind the leading pack with Katie by his side. Out of earshot with the rest he spoke softly to her.

'Is your dad going to be okay Katie? It's probably none of my business, but I was concerned for you when you had that little family meeting in private.'

Katie paused, thought for a few moments, sighed, then said, 'Look Dylan, if I tell you something in confidence, will you promise to keep it to yourself?'

'Of course I will hun. You can trust me.'

Katie looked at Dylan and saw only sincerity. She sighed again before speaking. 'The only reason we're here in Australia is because of my dad. He's not at all well really… he's got stomach cancer, and this is a big family holiday for us while we're all still together.'

Katie dabbed a tearful eye with a hankie she pulled out of her back pocket.

Dylan placed his arm around her shoulders. 'Sorry hun. Shouldn't have been so nosey.'

'It's alright,' sniffled Katie. 'You probably would have found out anyway. Just keep it to yourself that's all. Dad doesn't want a fuss and he's got enough to worry about at the moment, including being hunted down by every news hound in Eastern Australia.'

'Okay? …just between me and you then?' she added.

Dylan nodded.

Katie grabbed Dylan's hand and picked up her steps.' Come on, let's hurry and catch up with the rest. I can't wait to see Larry wearing make-up.'

NINETEEN

The show was good to go. It was agreed that Jenny would be the first to be interviewed. Sam would be the solo interviewer. It was a kind of reward.

The 'senate' was in place, a select gathering of rugby league personalities, legends past, present and yet to be. They were seated in a silent semi-circle behind Sam. Normally they would have been larking about, pinching cheap laughs at each other's expense and punching any available ribs. Tonight, it was solid sombre.

The show was opened by a pre-recorded video showing shots of Jamal in action, searing line-breaks, blistering tries, huge defensive hits, all followed by gushing and tearful tributes from team mates, comrades and coaches.

The studio cameras then moved in on a stern-faced Sam. Gravitas to the fore.

'We are here tonight to celebrate the short yet amazing

life of Jamal Jawai. A life far too short in fact and one so cruelly taken from us.'

The studio audience were invited to partake of a minute's applause and duly obliged. Most of the watching nation joined in.

Sam then turned to Jenny and introduced her as the valiant woman who had nurtured and encouraged the junior Jamal, stood by his side and by the side of the pitch as the young man had courageously fought his way through the junior ranks, fending off yobbish prop forwards, adversity, scepticism and indeed prejudice before his tremendous sporting ability and captivating character had finally won through.

Jenny slowly and studiously related the story of Jamal's early life, the brutal fight in his trial game which had earned him a junior contract when he was just twelve, the many hours of extra training in the dust and the puddles that blighted their shabby Outback village, the ensuing struggle to overcome poverty, family indifference, low esteem and self-doubt. Jamal had beaten them all only to lose his life in a freak accident as he approached the peak of his soaring career.

Sam nodded sympathetically and made empathetic humming noises throughout. He then asked Jenny to tell of the reasons she and Jamal were by the river on the night he died.

'We were there to see the asteroid again.'

'The one that's going to collide with earth?'

'Yes.'

Sam explained to his audience how Jenny had spotted the rogue rock in the starry heavens shimmering above an ancient and sacred Aboriginal site. The elders, he reported, had been wholly absorbed with the secrets of the stars long before Captain Cook had blundered into Botany Bay. He then proceeded to introduce Larry to his rapt audience and asked the English teenager to explain his remarkable role in this enthralling story.

Larry, nerves jangling, told of his internet friend Michael Berlingo, the amateur American astronomer and his dad Maurice, the monitors of the skies above Texas and their killer asteroid alert. He told of how he and Michael had found a newspaper story about Jamal's tweet on the internet, their response to it and how – to their amazement – Jamal had agreed to meet with Larry during their two-week family sojourn to Sydney. This was how these fickle turns of fate had led him to the riverside beach with Jenny and Jamal and an event which would probably stay with him for the rest of his life. Jenny, with tears in her eyes, reached over and took Larry's hand.

Sam then turned to the audience. He solemnly told how, in a previous programme, he had poked fun at Jamal's asteroid theory, of how they had invited him into the studio to raise a few cheap laughs at his friend's expense with scant regard for the consequences of their actions.

He asked for forgiveness. A nation collectively granted his request.

Sam then talked to George and Gaynor and Katie about their unintentional involvement in this frenetic family adventure, events which – mum and dad were only too willing to concede – had left them overwhelmed and quite distracted from the real reasons they had travelled to the other side of the world, to partake of sea, sunshine and several schooners of something toothsome. Bondi beach and its bars, George explained, with a resigned lift of his shoulders, continued to await their attention.

'Yeh, but you enjoyed the bungee jump, didn't ya?' piped up a young voice from the lower reaches of the Longworth gathering. 'That was on the holiday fun list wasn't it?' chirruped Dylan.

'Ah, our Australian friend,' smiled Sam with an eye to lightening the proceedings a tad.

'G'day!' exclaimed Dylan, pushing up the sleeves of his new denim shirt and manoeuvring his massive hair even higher up on his head. 'George was brilliant on the rope. A real trooper.'

'And what's been your role in this particular family saga Dylan? Did you know Jamal?'

'Well, kind of. I bumped into him outside the hotel when he met Larry on the night he died, and I've seen him in action on the telly a few times, but other than that, he was a bit of a stranger really.'

'So, how did you meet the Longworths?' asked Sam, wondering exactly why he'd agreed to allow this random hippie to appear on his show.

'They came and did the bungee jump where I work. It's called Jump the Shark up on the coast north of Sydney and it's totally fantastic. Loads of top NRL players have done it. They thought it was bloody great.'

That decided it for Sam. The hippie was swearing on his television show, name-dropping and had got away with a big gratis plug for his bungee jumping station. Bloody cheek. He'd soon shut him up.

'Dylan…although I believe that should really be Prestige?'

Dylan seemed to shrink into his chair, hair and all heading due south, his physical presence diminished with the utterance of a simple question, albeit one loaded with prior inside information. Sam allowed himself a brief sortie into smug mode before switching his attention back to the real, none self-promoting members of the family.

Katie, rather taken aback by the sudden and unexpected very public airing of Dylan's most embarrassing secret, decided that the conversation needed to be steered away from her suffering soul mate, back to the sombre if necessary. She explained that she and Dylan were now more than just good friends after meeting at the bungee jump and that he had joined them to support and help the family, particularly Dad who wasn't in the best of health. They were, after all, strangers in a foreign land while Dylan was very much on familiar territory. He was, she added, very much part of their holiday of a lifetime, in the true sense of the words.

Sam invited Larry back into the conversation again and asked him for more information about the asteroid, an anonymous piece of rock roaming around somewhere in space, yet a piece of rock that was the reason they were all together in a television studio with a gruesome, unwanted death on their hands.

Was there, Sam wanted to know, any scientific evidence supporting the rogue asteroid theory as put forward by the interested parties? Larry did a bit more nodding before revealing that Michael's dad had reported his findings to NASA, the American space organisation, who, he felt sure, were taking his claims most seriously. And now Jenny had joined in the debate, along with dear departed Jamal's input, those science boffins needed to sit up and take notice.

'Before we're all blown to bits?' asked Sam.

'Well, indeed,' replied Larry, glancing nervously across at his parents.

George frowned and shook his head, but deep down, his new-found admiration for his son surged and swirled.

TWENTY

NASA Professor David Emmerson picked up the ringing telephone on his desk, his tone crisp, polite and efficient.

The voice on the other end of the line belonged to Gregory H. Dowling, fellow American, professor, keen surfer and close colleague in all matters outer space, particularly inward-bound asteroids, threatening or otherwise.

Dowling was among the leadership of the eminent team who worked with the twin telescopes perched near the summit of Mount Mauna Kea on Hawaii. Just like the surfing waves on the remote Pacific Island, they were among the biggest and most powerful in the world. Dowling liked to tell people this when he mentioned his day off dalliance with the daring. But today there was no time to talk about his latest hanging ten or wipe-out. Dowling had responded to his colleague's request to follow his co-ordinates and peer deep into the heavens on the trail of a rogue rock he suspected was about to break its orbit and follow a course heading to Earth.

Professor Dowling reported that out in deep space, all wasn't as well as could be expected. An asteroid – very possibly a large one – looked suspiciously like it was on a wayward trajectory. It was still a bit early to say, but a near miss with Earth could not be ruled out. Neither could a direct hit. Both men were aware that the NASA asteroid investigation team was a mere cog in a chain of command that went all the way to the White House. They had a responsibility to report such findings to higher authorities. They were also aware of the need not to promulgate panic among nations, peoples and governments by making claims that could not be thoroughly substantiated and coming up with scary predictions that ultimately proved to be false.

'This is a tip-off put forward by an amateur star-gazer that we're investigating,' explained Professor Emmerson. 'Just one of the many who contact us, but this guy is persistent and confident. Apparently, there's an Aboriginal woman who's predicting much the same thing and she's been on national television in Australia to say so. Can't pretend to be sure about all these details, but I don't think we should close our eyes and hope this goes away.'

'I agree,' replied Professor Dowling. 'Give me a couple more days. I'll consult more colleagues, re-run the figures through even more expensive computers and we'll see where we are. I'll get back to you soon. Have you got any holiday left this this year, David? The surfing here is fantastic at the moment.'

'We'll be riding a tsunami the like of which modern man had never seen before if this lump of masonry pitches up on our doorstep,' replied Professor Emmerson in a menacing, low tone.

'Better get to work.'

TWENTY-ONE

Horizontal on his huge hotel bed, Larry was, as per usual, gazing at his phone, watching the Longworth television special for a third time.

It all still seemed surreal. The whole scenario possessed a dream-like quality, framing and highlighting events which should happen to other people, not a family of ordinaries from England on a foreign beach holiday because their dad was ill. He re-wound one of his interviews with Sam. He might have felt he was on another planet, but he was still glad the programme had loads of Larry in it. His reverie was broken by the door being pushed roughly opened by his dad who charged straight in. Sixteen-year-olds, apparently, were not deserving of a polite knock.

But George had urgent matters on his mind. He roughly shoved his son to one side of the bed, sat down heavily on the other end and started to bluster.

'I've just been out to buy a newspaper and have come back with about six different ones because we're all over the bloody lot of 'em. '

George picked up one of the newspapers, roughly shook it open and quickly flicked over the pages. 'Take a butchers at this lot,' he snorted. 'Pictures of you, me and the girls. Pictures of Jamal, Jamal playing rugby, Jamal looking muscular, Jamal looking gorgeous. None of Larry looking gorgeous. Pictures of Jenny and Jenny's sacred site. Pictures of teeth-laden crocodiles and a mean-looking river. Made-up pictures of great balls of fire soaring through the night sky, real pictures of twinkling stars, desperate showbiz stars, quotes, comments, cartoons, competitions, the whole nine yards. Then when I got back to the hotel, guess who was hiding behind that pillar and leapt out at me. Again.'

'That Reynolds guy. The Hyena,' replied Larry.

'Too bloody right.'

'What did he want?'

'He wanted to know why we had come to Australia in the first place.'

'What did you tell him?'

'I told him I'd suffered a badly dislocated sleeve playing full-back for Rochdale Hairnets several seasons ago and how I'd heard that the lager in New South Wales would be good for it. Then I told him to shove off. Let's see if he prints that pile of old bollocks.'

Larry chuckled softly and turned his head as the door was pushed open again, this time accompanied by a gentle tap, tap. Katie and Dylan walked in holding hands. Larry sighed and turned off his phone. His fourth viewing of the television programme with lots of him in it would have to wait.

'Have you seen the papers?' exclaimed Dylan. 'They've really gone to town on the story. There's only me not got a mention.'

'Here you are on page seven of this rag, picture as well,' replied George, throwing the paper untidily across the bed. 'I think they got your name wrong though.'

Dylan cursed softly under his breath, but still buried his head in the broadsheet.

'And what about all the social media sites?' added Katie excitedly. 'They're alive with scaremongering stories that an actual asteroid really is on its way. Apparently, a government minister in Canberra has had to issue some kind of official statement warning people not to panic because it's all a pile of cobblers. I don't think those were his exact words though. Or perhaps they were. This is Australia after all and they seem to like to tell it as it is. The other day, I saw a police sign at the side of the road warning about the dangers of boozing then getting behind the wheel and it read... "if you drink and drive, you're a bloody fool."

'I've never seen anything like that next to the M1.'

TWENTY-TWO

P hil Reynolds roughly pushed open the newspaper office door, stamped across the editorial floor and irritably kicked the chair under his desk.

He was not in the best of moods.

Following his initial sensational scoop – first hack on the scene just a few hours after Jamal Jawai's macabre death in the jaws of a crocodile – Reynolds had slipped well down the journos' league table of insufferably large egos. Near the relegation zone in fact.

And it was all the fault of that bloody Sam Runceman. The former rugby league player turned media personality had stolen all his thunder and had seemingly cornered the market in all matters Longworth. His despised rival had lured every one of the family on to his pathetic rugby league magazine show to dole out exclusive interviews and so enthral a nation. There was even an emotional Aboriginal woman thrown in for good measure. This had left the rest of the chasing pack – including the venomous Reynolds – picking up meagre crumbs cast from the heavily laden banqueting table of Sam the Man.

And not only that, but the upstart Runceman had also managed to shut down all lines of communication with the Longworth clan. Reynolds had tried all the standard tricks of his greasy trade, ambushes in the street, the pestering of hotel staff, the bribing of petty officials, but still had little to show for all his efforts. Confronting the dad on the street had produced a quote of sorts, but Reynolds had soon worked out that George was enjoying a cheap chortle at his expense. Rochdale Hairnets indeed.

Reynolds needed a new angle, a fresh story, a new line to move him up the pecking order in the vicious dingo-eat-dingo world that was the Sydney media jungle. He grabbed himself a large coffee, booted up his desk computer and replayed Runceman's television show. Despite his professional loathing and resentment, he suspected there might be a half-hidden lead he could pick up on, a small window of opportunity to slither through.

He listened and watched as Sam the Man's gushing guests went through their stories, Jenny, Larry, the parents and Katie. Then this rather unexplained hippie had got himself involved, grabbing himself a big free plug for his bungee jump business, a touch of cheek which had seemed to irk Runceman somewhat. This rather pleased Reynolds. Then he listened to Katie defend her hippie boyfriend, adding that he and the family were all supporting dad, George, who was "not in the best of health".

Reynolds frowned, sat up straight and paid closer attention. He carried on watching and noticed that little more had been made of this small, but important revelation. Indeed, it had never mentioned again. He re-wound the programme and listened to the hippie – who was apparently either called Dylan or Prestige – grab his free plug. The bungee jump was called "Jump the Shark", and it was probably situated up the coast on the way to Queensland, but even if he was wrong, he could soon find it on the internet.

Reynolds paused the programme and deliberated. All the Longworth family knew who he was and had already made it quite clear that they wouldn't speak to him. Indeed, they seemed to regard him as public enemy number one, two and three.

But Dylan had never met him. He wouldn't have a clue who he was, let alone that he was a journalist on the prowl. And Reynolds knew where he lived, well worked anyway, which was enough. The hippie seemed to know all the Longworth family pretty well and quite possibly knew what was wrong with George. Nothing trivial he hoped.

Reynolds shut down his computer with a flourish and allowed himself a sly, smug grin.

He was going in. And he already had a plan.

▼

"Jump the Shark" was indeed on the coast road heading north out of Sydney. A mere two-hour drive. Reynolds had driven further to go to a party.

A search on its internet site had revealed that the bungee jump boasted a bar where the successful survivors could toast their daring. It was called the "Buck Stops Here." Neat name mused Reynolds. It stayed open long after the last customer had been dipped head first into the menacing waters at the bottom of the gorge. Reynold regarded this as perfect for his plan. The last jump was 7.00pm. Reynolds would be there in time to watch it.

He drove quickly and determinedly along the scenic highway and arrived at the time he'd aimed for. He left his car in the designated car park near the jump bridge and watched the last customer of the day climb the steps to the launch platform. He placed the worst sunglasses in the world on top of his nose and squinted skywards into the dipping sun as a teenage girl in a pink swimsuit was being attached to a large elastic rope by a hippie with hair all over the parish. Reynolds recognised Dylan immediately. He watched the girl plunge head first towards the water and spring upwards feet from the surface. Two youths rowed out to detach and collect her before Dylan shouted something undecipherable and hauled the rope back on to the platform. Reynolds waited several minutes before he gassed back his hair, straightened his suit, checked he had plenty of dollars stashed in his bill fold and sashayed nonchalantly into the "Buck Stops Here".

Dylan was sitting at a side table with two other guys about his age. They were all drinking large vessels of lager. There was a middle-aged couple with two teenage sons on the other side of the room – presumably earlier customers – and a barman who was looking distinctly bored. Reynolds approached the bar, issued a cheery greeting and wafted his face with a fan made up of several dollar bills.

'Evening mate,' he chirruped. 'Is it okay if I get a drink? I've not done the jump, but I might be tempted some time.'

The barman nodded, and Reynolds ordered a small shandy, heavy on the lemonade. He asked the barman his name and then asked him if he would like a drink too. On him of course. Bruce smiled, thanked him and pulled himself a cooking lager.

'Is the owner in?' Reynolds asked.

'No, but the deputy manager is. He's sitting over there. The guy with the long hair. He's called Dylan. Can I ask who wants him and what you want?'

'The name's John, John Taylor. I was just passing through and spotted this place and I like the look of it, so I was wondering if I could perhaps make a block booking for me and my mates. Sounds like it might be fun.'

'I'll take you over.'

'Okay, if you could introduce me and then bring all three of them drinks, said Reynolds. 'Large premium lagers please.'

Bruce nodded, shrugged his shoulders and led Reynolds to the table, unwittingly sliding a peckish weasel into an unwary rabbit warren. The barman introduced the newcomer to Dylan, Spider and Spudgun who returned semi-amiable grunts of greeting.

'This is John Taylor,' Bruce said. 'He's interested in making a block booking. And he's buying us all a drink.'

Bruce left to pull the strong lagers and Reynolds pulled up a chair.

'Hi guys, great to meet you. I've just watched the young girl dive off the launch platform. I thought it was fantastic. Something I think I'd really like to do. One of my mates is thirty in a few weeks and there's a whole gang of us getting together to celebrate his birthday. This place looks ideal.

Scare them all to death and then boast all about it in here with several schooners of the strong stuff.'

Bruce approached the table with three fizzing lagers on a tray and placed them in front of his colleagues.

'John's paid for these,' he said. 'He's bought me one too.'

Reynolds raised his small glass of shandy and toasted their good health. His three slightly bemused guests drank deeply and returned his best wishes.

'Okay guys', gushed Reynolds, 'Tell me all about how this operation works. Then perhaps we can do a deal.'

For the next forty minutes, Dylan, Spider and Spudgun described in some detail how they ran "Jump the Shark". Bookings, safety, health checks, the measuring of the special elasticated ropes in tandem with the weight of the customer were all explained with some gusto while Bruce, on the persistent insistence of Reynolds, continued to ferry copious amounts of high strength lager to the table. He met with little objection. Dylan did wonder why this strange bloke kept buying them drinks, and concluded it was part of a plan to secure a discount on a block booking. He wasn't right.

The more the drinks flowed, the more the three amigos enthused about their own vital roles and their colourful experiences on and about the water. The more inebriated they became the more anecdotal they got, team guffaws to the fore amid embroidered yarns, including the one about the fat bloke who plunged head first into the water right up to the waist. Dylan's fault.

They talked about the customers who lost their nerve on the edge of the platform. Despite Dylan's sturdy rope work and purring reassurances, there were several instances of clients who took one peep over the precipice and headed straight back to the bar. And it was often cocky young men whose bottle went AWOL so close to the point of no return. They would climb the steps full of swagger and bravura, bragging to their mates about the sweet swallow dive they would execute only to suffer a crisis of confidence seconds before taking the plunge.

Women and older men, they collectively agreed, were made of the tough stuff.

And on they prated, the drinks flowed, the stories became more outlandish, the atmosphere heady and relaxed, Reynolds going with the flow and sticking with a couple of small, sensible shandies. There was a pause in proceedings while Spudgun and Spider stumbled into the sit-downs to banish the first three of six pints of strong lager.

Reynolds the Hyena spotted his chance and slinked in. He stared a slightly swaying Dylan straight in the eye and asked, 'Don't I know you from somewhere mate? Haven't I seen you before?'

'Don't think so,' slurred Dylan. 'I've never seen you before.'

Reynolds fixed his fake face with a concentrating/ intelligent look and furrowed his brow.

'You seem familiar to me… where do I recognise you from? You've not been on television recently have you?'

Dylan's half-stupefied brain filled with pride and pleasure. His fifteen minutes of fame on Sam the Man's show had been more like fifteen seconds, yet here was this great bloke John Taylor who had both recognised and remembered him. And bought him a boatload of ale. Was this the finest chap he'd ever met?

Dylan did his best to appear modest but wasn't sure he made a decent fist of it.

'I have been on television actually, just a couple of days ago…'

'Stop', interrupted Reynolds, raising his hand. 'Let me think…I think it's going to come to me.'

Reynolds conjured up another thoughtful, memory-searching false face, accompanied by much brow-furrowing and chin-stroking. He suddenly plonked his glass heavily on the table and exclaimed, 'I've got it! You were the guy on that Sam Runceman show, with the English family who got caught up in the death of that well-known rugby league player.' Reynolds paused, frowned and lied ruefully…'so well-known that I can't remember his name.'

'Jamal Jawai', chipped in Dylan, helpfully, 'they all believed that an asteroid is heading towards earth as well.'

'That's right, yeh, I remember that as well now', added Reynolds, slowly and deliberately. 'Do you know, I've never met anyone who's been on television before. Let me shake you by the hand young man. I never thought I was going to meet a celebrity tonight.'

Dylan's already inflated ego was close to bursting as Spider and Spudgun spluttered their way back and re-joined them at the table.

Reynolds cursed under his breath – he had still not got what he wanted – but outwardly was all smiles and generosity personified as he looked over in vain to summon an absent barman.

'I assume you guys saw young Dylan here on television', barked Reynolds to the returning drinkers. 'You're working with a star.'

Spider and Spudgun nodded in vague agreement before draining their glasses and looking over at their benefactor with beseeching faces. Reynolds forced a reluctant smile, picked up their empty vessels and walked over to the bar himself. Bruce popped up from a cellar trap door behind the bar. Reynolds ordered three more lagers and as they were pulled was pleased to see a solo Dylan wobble over to join him. He suspected the young man was in the market for some more flattery and he was right.

'Did you watch the whole programme then John?', asked Dylan.

'Yep, most of it. I found it all a bit sad really. Such a shame about the death of that rugby player and the family seemed to be going through such a hard time as well.'

'How do you mean?' asked Dylan, now feeling decidedly drunk.

'Well, the teenage son was there by the river when that Jamal was killed by that croc and didn't someone say that the dad was ill as well? I hope it's nothing serious. You must have got to know the family pretty well Dylan. How are they coping with all this misfortune? Jeez, they're supposed to be on holiday having a good time, not putting up with all this misery.'

'Yeh, they came on holiday for a big treat because their dad's quite ill. It doesn't seem fair really.'

'Is he really bad then? Nothing too serious I hope.'

'He's got stomach cancer. I don't think it's too great for him.'

A little bell jangling at the back of Dylan's addled brain told him that George's illness was supposed to be a secret. But this was a total random stranger he had told. There was no connection to the family. No harm could come of it. No way. Everything was sweet.

'Jeez, that must be tough on those guys,' gushed Reynolds. 'How long's dad got?'

'Not a clue,' replied Dylan, 'but they're only here in Australia for a couple of weeks.'

Reynolds smiled inwardly. He had enough. He picked up two of the three glasses and invited Dylan to carry his own drink over and join him back at the table where Spider and Spudgun slavered and slouched. Dylan picked up the glass of lager – his eighth – and followed in the wake of his new hero. It was more of a weave than a walk.

'Now, about this block booking,' said Reynolds when they were all back around the table. 'There will be about twelve of us. Can you fix me up with a sweet discount Dylan?'

Dylan dragged one of his business cards out of his back pocket and handed it over. 'Give me a ring in the next couple of days John. I'll sort you out a great deal. And thanks for a fantastic night. It's been a real hoot.'

Spider and Spudgun formed a small chorus and expressed their wholehearted agreements. Reynolds climbed to his feet and shook hands with his three new friends. Or should that be unfortunate victims? He then bade them a final farewell and walked out into the fallen shades of night.

On the way to his car, he slipped his hand into the inside pocket of his jacket. The red light on his digital voice recorder told him it was still functioning correctly. He had surreptitiously powered it up on the way to the bar before he had spoken to Dylan on his own. He looked around furtively before playing back the last few minutes. Dylan's voice was slightly slurred, but what he was saying was loud and clear. Reynolds re-pocketed the recorder and started the car engine. His plan had worked perfectly. It had cost him a few more beers than he had originally intended, but the newspaper would stump up for those.

He sparked up his phone, speed-dialled "the desk" and told them the front page was all his. He was coming in.

The pecking order of big-headed journos in the big bad city was about to undergo a re-shuffle.

TWENTY-THREE

There was a bell going off in George's head and it was annoying him.

He turned his head on his pillow and glanced at the digital clock on his bedside table. It read 7.13am and next to it the hotel's internal telephone was ringing. George pulled the pillow over his head and hoped it would go away. It didn't. He reached a reluctant arm out of the warm duvet, grabbed the telephone, dragged it over and barked 'yes' down it, the irritation in his voice loud and clear.

A woman's hesitant voice said, 'Er, Mr Longworth? It's Heather here on front reception. I'm terribly sorry to disturb you, especially so early in the morning, but there have been so many telephone calls for you that I'm at a loss as to what to do.'

'Who on earth wants me?' mumbled George from behind half a pillow.

'Well, I think it's the press.'

'What do that lot want again?'

'I wouldn't have a clue. What do you want me to tell them?'

'Tell them all to bugger off…er, sorry Heather, I mean, tell them to go away.'

'It's alright Mister Longworth, I'll tell them to bugger off.'

▼

Dylan woke up with a head like Birkenhead.

He had foolishly listened to a sloshed Spudgun and stayed in the "Buck Stops Here" after his beloved free beer provider had taken his leave. Two more large lagers had pushed his lager tally for the night into double figures. He had been well drunk.

Now he felt his brain had been cast adrift from its moorings.

Dylan crawled out of bed into the bathroom. He looked at his face in the mirror above the sink and shuddered. His eyes were bloodshot and carrying twin luggage. His tongue throbbed. The three-day growth on his face was bordering on standard wino trim. He groaned and wobbled uncertainly over to the lounge window, trying to piece together the events of a most unusual night. There were plenty of blanks, but he certainly remembered the guy doling out the free beers. He pulled open the curtains and peered out into the harsh early morning light.

'Oh no, tell me it's not bloody true,' he wailed, anguish causing his voice to crack and break. He stared unbelievingly at his own car which was parked untidily on the communal car park outside his flat. He had driven home, and he didn't remember doing that. It wasn't far, but if the police had stopped him, he would have been chucked into prison for ever. Dylan stepped gingerly back to his bed, sat on it and placed his head in his hands wondering how he could possibly have been so stupid. He looked at the clock by his side and sighed wearily. He was already late for work.

Dylan dressed hurriedly, set off in his motor – possibly still over the limit – and quickly realised that he desperately needed hydration. He felt mighty rough. He drew to a halt in a parking bay outside a 7-Eleven shop at the side of the road. As he headed for the entrance, an 'A' frame advertising board near the door grabbed his attention. On the top it read: "The Sydney Bugle". Underneath, in large bold characters, it read: "Exclusive: TV Asteroid Dad Dying of Cancer."

Dylan paused, puzzled, read it again and talked to himself. 'That must be Katie's dad, George. He's not going to be happy that's leaked out. I wonder how that happened?'

At the counter, Dylan ordered a carton of fresh orange juice and a large bottle of still water. As the woman walked away to bring them, Dylan noticed a stack of "Bugles" on the side of the serving surface. He pulled the top one over to him. The front-page banner headline read the same as the blurb on the "A" frame: "TV Asteroid Dad Dying of Cancer." Alongside was a large picture by-line which read: "World Exclusive by Phil Reynolds."

Underneath the words was a picture of John Taylor.

Dylan stared at the picture in disbelief. It was definitely John Taylor, the great bloke who had bought him all those beers last night. So, what on earth was his picture doing on

186

the front of the newspaper? Why wasn't it a picture of this Phil Reynolds guy?

Dylan unfurled the folded paper and quickly scanned the words under the splash. The "Asteroid Dad" was indeed George. Lower down the piece lurked his picture, alongside shots of Gaynor, Larry, Katie, Jamal Jawai, a hungry crocodile and an unfeasibly fake asteroid. Dylan started to read the story quickly. The sixth paragraph stated, "A source close to the family last night revealed that the English dad at the heart of the Jamal Jawai tragedy is suffering from stomach cancer. The source confirmed that the prognosis wasn't good and that they would be going home soon."

A wave of horrified understanding suddenly swept over Dylan. This was immediately followed by an even larger wave of nausea. He took another look at the by-line photograph of John Taylor and now only saw Phil Reynolds, Phil Reynolds the Hyena, the conman, the trickster, the number one bastard of all bastard journalists. Dylan suddenly felt quite ill. He already felt ill enough as it was, but now his queasy stomach was a mosh pit of fear, loathing, anger and resentment, all coagulating and curdling with the sour, stale-ale bile already on the swirl down below.

A woman clutching orange juice and water appeared behind the counter and looked quizzically at an ashen young man staring into the mid-distance and saying nothing.

'Are you alright sweetie?' she asked.

Dylan looked at her, turned and fled from the shop.

Three yards from his car door he was violently sick on the asphalt.

▼

George and Gaynor went down to breakfast early. George had not returned to sleep after his rude awakening, so had sat up in bed and whinged at his wife.

They were making their way across the front of the reception desk when Heather waved them over.

'Would you mind popping into the back office, just for a couple of minutes?' she asked, smiling disarmingly.

George and Gaynor frowned, but nodded and followed Heather into the room. She turned and stood by the photocopier with a newspaper in her hand and said, 'I realise this is probably none of my business, but I think you need to take a look at this.'

She handed them a copy of the Sydney Bugle.

Gaynor and George gaped at the front page together, united in dismay and disbelief.

'How the bloody hell did the Hyena find out?' demanded George. 'There was only us guys knew about the cancer. We said we'd keep it in the family and that's exactly what we've done. Has all this publicity turned our Larry into a super-grass?'

Gaynor shook her head and led George into the breakfast room. Over a pot of tea, she read the story slowly and carefully.

'Nowhere, apart from in the headline, does it say that you're dying and there are no direct quotes from anyone. Most of the story is just a re-hash of all the stuff that's been printed before, Jamal's death, the asteroid theory, blah, blah, blah. But there is one fact that they've got just right, a fact which surely proves that someone in the know has leaked the information.'

'What's that then?' asked George stirring his tea and wishing he could have sugar in it. And whisky.

'They've not said that you've just got cancer, but specifically stomach cancer, which of course is spot on. They surely haven't guessed that. Someone must have told them.'

'But who?'

'I don't know George. These newspaper people seem to have ways and means of finding things out which are completely beyond the likes of me and you. We may never find out who the source is.'

George grunted, stood up, and repaired to the buffet table to grab himself a bowlful of shavings off a rabbit hutch floor with the droppings still in it.

As he spooned his luxury muesli, Katie suddenly appeared at his side. She also had a copy of the Sydney Bugle.

'I got this at the reception Dad. Have you seen it?'

'Yes, I bloody well have. Heather gave us a copy. Somebody's grassed us up, that's for sure and I'd dearly like to know who it is.'

There was a telling silence before Katie lifted her head and spoke.

'I've just had a phone call. I know who it is who told that Reynolds guy about your illness Dad,' Katie confessed, slowly and sullenly.

'You do?' replied George, patent surprise in his voice. 'It was that quisling brother of yours wasn't it?'

'It's not Larry dad. He wouldn't do anything like that.'

'Who then?' demanded George. 'Nobody else knew.'

'I knew,' mumbled Katie.

'You!' exclaimed George.

'Is Mum having breakfast over there?' said Katie, turning and nodding towards the dining room.

'Yes, she is.'

'I'll get some coffee, then I'll come over and join you both. I'll explain everything.'

▼

Gaynor and George sat in stunned silence over cold slices of toast and congealing eggs as Katie delivered chapter and verse.

She detailed her recent phone call from a distraught Dylan explaining all about surreal events in the "Buck Stops Here" the previous night. The gin-trap as set by the Hyena – or should that read lager-trap – his subsequent cunning and Dylan's unfortunate revelation about George's illness were handed centre stage. But Katie confessed that she too had to accept a portion of the blame. Her voice and head both lowered as she delivered the shame-tinged truth.

'I told Dylan that dad had stomach cancer when we were at the television studios. He was sworn to secrecy and I'm sure he wouldn't have breathed a word to anyone. But ten pints of lager and the trickery of that Reynolds guy was clearly too much for him. He's so sorry Mum and Dad. He feels terrible and so do I. He's gone to work in a right old state. I'm worried he'll be jumping off that top stage without a rope attached.'

'There won't be any need for that,' said George. 'It's quite clear that these press guys over here have ways of getting the stories they want, and they don't mind who gets trampled underfoot on the way. There was me thinking that it's us gullible English folk who are particularly vulnerable, but that young Dylan, well, he's as Australian as a Vegemite sandwich and he was well and truly fooled. I feel sorry for the kid.'

Katie reached over the breakfast table and gently took her father's hand. 'Thanks for being so understanding Dad. Dylan will be so relieved.'

'That's okay hun. Just tell him it's his round.'

TWENTY-FOUR

Professor Greg H. Dowling was a man with weighty matters on his mind.

Deep in his science room on top of Mount Manau Kea in Hawaii, his eyes flicked from screen to screen, scanning the array of computers which were linked to two of the most potent telescopes in the world.

The telescopes were trained on the area of deep space linked to the reports of a large rogue asteroid with a mind of its own. Professor Dowling had dedicated many hours to his investigations and he didn't particularly care for the conclusion he was reaching. He picked up the telephone to speak to Professor David Emmerson, his colleague at NASA HQ in America.

Prof Emmerson nodded sagely as his colleague outlined his fears and findings. The mutual conclusion was that this particularly chunky asteroid had already veered away from its orbit while the risk of it heading towards earth was clear and present. A rough estimate calculated it was hurtling through space at about 20 kilometres per second. This was a rock in a rush. The chances of a collision with earth were, as yet, too hard to calculate with any degree of accuracy, but there was one certainty – there was a chance. Higher authorities had to be informed, ignoring or concealing the evidence the scientists had already collated would be grave folly.

Professor Emmerson was only too aware that the chain of responsibility for reporting such a serious concern led all the way to the White House, underlying the gravity of the situation. Military chiefs, top FBI brass, leading government agencies in the USA and all over the world would have to be informed. This wasn't only America's problem, it was a problem for the planet. How much of a problem remained to be seen, but inertia was not an option.

TWENTY-FIVE

In the White House press office, the pressure was on.

And the person with the largest onus of responsibility bearing down on her young shoulders was Laura Pitt, the director of strategic communications, directly answerable to the President.

An earlier top-level briefing involving some of the highest-ranking officials in the federal government and its agencies, the FBI, CIA, Homeland Security and many others, merely served to confirm the importance of her role. The highly secret meeting had discussed worst case scenarios: A direct strike from a large asteroid, especially on a large, densely populated country, would result in mass death and destruction, the certain breakdown of vast tracts of civilised society, famine and pestilence, fearful words bandied about with alarming readiness. Even an asteroid strike in a remote part of the earth could still cause mass annihilation, the subsequent explosion the catalyst for a firestorm on the planet surface, thousands of tons of flaming debris soaring into the upper atmosphere, creating nature's equivalent of a nuclear winter. High-level layers of ash, soot and smoke would blot out the sun, day no longer following night, crops failing, fresh water contaminated and undrinkable, huge, highly destructive tsunamis, fire-breathing volcanoes... a scenario even worse than a Cliff Richard concert and the human race completely unable to cope. More than 60 million years ago, dinosaurs hadn't coped at all well with their asteroid. They all died.

Laura's demanding remit was to produce a press release, the aim of which was two-fold. Firstly, to warn of a perceived threat, secondly, not to create global panic. A few easy words to trip off the tongue, but in reality, a task that would test her every journalistic skill while the finished piece would have to be signed off by the man in the Big Chair. Laura was chewing the end of her pencil long before the meeting had ended.

But an hour after the debate was over, her words were finished. They read: "American space scientists have detected unusual activity in an asteroid belt visible from Earth by telescope. Early calculations indicate that a rogue asteroid has left its original orbit and could pass close to Earth. There is no evidence to suggest that a collision will happen, but this responsible government believes it has a duty to inform all citizens of the situation. We also expect those same citizens to behave responsibly, not to panic, listen to official government statements and understand that everything will be done to keep you fully informed."

The President signed it off without too much ado, and the missive was sent electronically to all major news agencies around the world.

It didn't work.

It worked in as much as the world was alert to the threat of a nuclear fireball crashing into Mother Earth. Where it failed was the wholly unexpected levels of over-reaction and life-changing decisions taken by so many people in so many nations.

Shelters were dug, supermarket shelves were emptied, people abandoned secure jobs, emptied bank accounts and fled cities for the country where they hoarded money, food and water. Crime increased, gun sales increased, sexual activity increased. People skipped work, long-term travel plans were abandoned, holidays cancelled, long-lost relatives looked up. Protests and demonstrations paraded the streets of big cities, why, no-one really knew. Alcohol and other drug sales soared. Government ministers did much hand-wringing and made lots of reassuring noises. Still the world seethed with unease, nowhere more so than on the Eastern seaboard of Australia. Here, the Longworth's unwanted family fame ratcheted up from national to world-wide. This was a fascinating family who had predicted the arrival of this asteroid long before the space boffins had hit the right buttons. Jenny's role created a huge interest in all matters Aboriginal while Larry suddenly found himself in more demand than his dad.

He was secretly quite pleased about this.

There was a young man in America who was also particularly animated.

Larry turned on his smart phone and, as suspected, fell upon an array of missed calls from Michael Berlingo in Texas. More a bombardment really. Larry called him up and wondered if modern technology would ever invent a filter for uncontrollable excitement.

His friend was like a human exclamation mark on springs. 'Oh boy Larry. We're all going to be famous. You're famous already and now the media guys over here have tracked down dad and are virtually parked in our driveway twenty-four seven. I was always confident he was right. Fame at last. It feels just great.'

'But according to you, we're all going to die horrible deaths. Take your pick from fire, flood or famine. Fame isn't going to save your soul my American friend,' retorted Larry.

'Yeh, right, but the scientists will come up with a plan to save us. Those NASA guys are smart cookies.'

'Let's hope so', replied Larry before the connection dropped out and Michael disappeared.

'The smart cookies can't even make a telephone that works properly,' Larry mumbled to himself.

TWENTY-SIX

At the University of Coogee Bay in down town Sydney, post-graduate oncologist researcher Dr. Saul Sorensen was feeling rather impressed with himself.

After years of extensive study and experiments in the lab, the clinician believed that the success he had sought for so long was within touching distance. His research work had been focused on the treatment and possible cure for stomach cancer, one of his many trials strongly suggesting that the affected cells could be attacked and even eradicated by a genetically modified virus.

He sensed he was on the brink of a break-through but needed two things: a willing human guinea pig and public awareness of the medical benefits his work may provide. Like most of the population of Australia, Dr. Sorensen had taken on board the surreal stories surrounding the gruesome death-by-crocodile fate of rugby league star Jamal Jawai. The tendrils of this particular yarn had travelled far and wide. But when he also learned of the plight of Englishman George Longworth – a man wholly embroiled in this remarkable story – several light bulbs came on at once, a couple of them Sydney Harbour spotlights.

Here was a man at the beating heart of public interest who had stomach cancer. Hero doc would step in, save this poor soul's life – even if he was a Pom – and in turn receive massive state funding and universal acclaim for his pioneering work.

Dr. Sorensen decided he needed to stop dreaming that he was Crocodile Dundee's smarter brother and picked up the telephone.

TWENTY-SEVEN

George and Gaynor took seats either side of a small table in the corner of a quiet down town bar and clinked their glasses together.

They had deliberately chosen an anonymous back street hostelry because, as George was only too happy to complain about, ordinary folk would recognise him in the main streets. They would stare, point and whisper, George usually able to pick out the few pertinent words that would paint the whole picture... Jamal Jawai, asteroid, cancer etc.

'We've been here for a week and I was wondering exactly when this holiday's going to start,' remarked Gaynor, sipping her gin and tonic.

'I know exactly what you mean. It hasn't exactly been relaxing has it?' replied George, wincing slightly as he took the top off his lager. 'We've been too busy dealing with international celebrity status. Fame and fortune without the fortune.'

Gaynor had been to the bar to order the drinks and the young barmaid had taken little notice of her other than to remark that she was English and a long way from home. But as Gaynor and George chatted, the barmaid was joined by an older man and after some conspiratorial chat, the pointing and whispering began…Jamal Jawai, asteroid, cancer etc. George glanced over, saw the pair looking at him and knew he was the object of their interest. He took another drink of his lager, but seconds after he had swallowed, George suddenly turned away from his wife, folded his body at the waist and vomited copiously on to the floor.

Gaynor cried out, rushed to George's side and placed a hand on his back, her husband continuing to wretch and heave, his eyes filled with tears, his whole body seemingly convulsed and shuddering. Eventually, the vomiting stopped, and George gingerly straightened his body and raised his head.

'Bloody Australian lager,' he whined. 'It's like drinking sheep dip.'

Gaynor looked at her husband anxiously. 'Do you really think it's the beer George? It's never had such an effect on you in the past.'

George lowered his head. 'No, not really,' he replied quietly. 'If I'm being honest, I reckon it's a combination of the cancer and all the stress of live television appearances, newspaper headlines and journalists lurking around most corners.'

'Have you been keeping up with your medication?'

'Yes', replied George slightly irritably. 'But the doctor did warn there would be side effects, including nausea and vomiting and this is exactly what's happening. He also said that it was important to relax and not stress about stuff, but that's proving almost impossible with this lot going on.'

Gaynor placed her arms around her husband and hugged him hard, her head on his shoulders, salty tears seeping into his new holiday t-shirt. When she eventually looked up the barmaid was standing by their side with a mop and bucket in her hands and a concerned look on her face.

▼

Sam the Man was in the offices of the television studio, checking emails and tinkering with the script for the next show later in the week.

No matter how diligently he worked, the new programme would never match the Longworth special, the fall-out from which was still filling newspaper columns and fuelling frenzied speculation on social media sites throughout the country and beyond.

The telephone on his desk trilled and Sam's huge right hand hefted the handset to his ear. The receptionist told him that a doctor called Saul Sorensen was on the line and wondered if he could speak with him. It was to do with George Longworth she informed him and was she to put him through?

Sam agreed and for the next five minutes listened attentively to the clinician's plan. He nodded a lot. In return for persuading George to undergo his pioneering cancer treatment, Sam could have the exclusive story for his television show which in turn would provide the doctor with the publicity he sought. 'Doesn't that make everyone a winner?' posited Dr. Sorensen as he summed up his proposals.

'I think George is a bit fed up with being the centre of attention,' said Sam. 'He was all over the front of the Sydney Bugle a couple of days ago and they'll be on his back again if we go public with this.'

'But hopefully the treatment will do him a lot of good, perhaps even cure him, wouldn't the benefits outweigh the downsides?' argued the medic.

'Possibly,' replied Sam. 'There's only one way to find out. We'll have to ask George and his family. Ultimately the decision is theirs.'

▼

Sam invited George and his family to meet him in their hotel front reception room, Dylan also invited. The hapless hippie had been forgiven his indiscretion and as he, and now several million others, knew about George's illness anyway, George raised no objection. Katie would also be pleased.

Dylan shuffled over to the bar for the drinks, ordering himself a lime and soda, a rather sensible choice under the circumstances he thought. Lager was banned from his life… for the time being at least. George had also opted for a soft drink, but for entirely different reasons.

Sam, the effervescent host as ever, shook hands, kissed cheeks and slapped backs. He announced with a flourish how a special foundation trust in memory of Jamal had been set up. The aim of the trust was to provide financial support for promising young Aboriginal rugby league players, of which there were plenty. But many, like Jamal, came from impoverished backgrounds and most didn't have mentors like Jenny to help them along the way. Pots of money had poured in from many sources and it was all down to the Longworths and their heroic television appearance. Sam, wearing a weak smile born of melancholy, assured all that Jamal would have approved.

Then he called the room to order and informed his rapt audience of five that he had rather a big surprise to announce. This, he agreed, would be tricky to believe, but George and his family may indeed end up thanking dago journo Phil Reynolds for tracking down Dylan, pouring several pints of wicked-strength lager down his neck and duping him mercilessly before penning that over-sensationalised front-page piffle about George dying of stomach cancer. Yes, it was difficult to come to terms with, but the family may still owe a debt of gratitude to that double-crossing, half-breed son of a gout-ridden hyena.

Sam paused for dramatic effect and possibly acclaim. He was rather enjoying himself.

'It is said that all publicity is good publicity,' he wittered on. 'And even in the case of half-baked, ill-gotten stories written by that complete and utter bastard Reynolds, this would also seem to be true.'

Sam surveyed a collection of baffled faces.

'Get to the point Sam,' sighed Gaynor.

'Yeh, right, sorry about that, prattled on a bit there, guys. Okay, so here's the really amazing bit. I've received an important telephone call from a university medical guy called doctor Saul Sorensen. He's in a lab on the other side of Sydney doing research into the treatment of stomach cancer. He's seen the newspapers and watched the television, so he knows all about George. Now he reckons he's on the brink of some big breakthrough and wants to test his new wonder drug on a human victim, no, sorry patient. He also wants the trial to attract plenty of publicity so needs a guinea pig who's big in the news at the moment.'

Sam again paused for the implication to hit home before adding, 'Is there anybody here in the room who you think might fit the bill?'

Even Dylan stared at George who in turn stared helplessly into mid-space. He knew he should have gone to Bournemouth.

'And what kind of publicity does he want?' asked George wearily.

'Just an appearance on one of my fabulous shows alongside you of course George', added Sam. 'A small price to pay surely. Let's not forget that the doc is talking a possible cure here guys.'

'How long will the treatment take? 'asked Gaynor.

'About a month.'

'You've overlooked one big flaw in the plan,' said George. 'I'm going home later this week.'

An uneasy silence descended. Gaynor looked at Katie, Katie looked at Larry and Larry looked at his feet. It was Gaynor who eventually spoke.

'There have been a few, erm, developments on the going home front George. We've not told you yet, but now seems as good a time as any. Our flight back to England has been put on hold, delayed, postponed...I don't really know the best way to describe it.'

'Why?'

'Much of it is to do with this asteroid worry that's all over the world, so it's all our own fault. Airlines are in disarray because so many passengers have cancelled travel plans while thousands of others want to come home early. A lot of pilots have walked out because of the insecurity of it all. Their logic is hard to argue with. If we're all going to die in a raging inferno, then why should they carry on working to help others? They'd rather help themselves. They're also afraid of the threat to flights in the air even if Larry's bloody asteroid just zooms by fairly close. There's so much turmoil and uncertainty that normal flight schedules have gone out of the window and our trip home is on hold indefinitely until this lot has blown over and we all get back to leading normal lives. Hopefully.'

'Bloody hell and set fire to it. I need to talk to Bernard,' burbled George.

TWENTY-EIGHT

First, George had to talk to Esme and Harry, his neighbours back home, so cajoled Larry into firing up his laptop, son staying alongside dad as abacus man accessed the airwaves.

Esme answered the Skype call on her lap-top and greeted George with a barrage of exclamations, gasps and questions. She expressed utter amazement at her friends' sudden and wholly unexpected rise to international fame, their television appearance which had popped up all over the world – especially since the asteroid warning had proved to be true – all featuring the ordinary family next door. Or least the family they had once thought were ordinary.

George dipped into his reserves of patience and answered all Esme's questions with as much enthusiasm as he could muster before spotting his opportunity and asking one himself, 'Can I speak to Bernard please Esme?'

Esme, still slightly bemused by her neighbour's canine eccentricities, placed the laptop on the sofa and ushered the hound in front of the screen. Bernard saw his master and best mate, slobbered on the floor and thumped his tail with a flourish.

'Bernard, my old mate, how the hell are you?' said George.

The dog's tail beat a bit faster.

'Have you heard about all this mind-blowing stuff that's been going on down here? We appeared on television like I told you about, mentioned the killer asteroid theory and now it seems that it's true. The bloody thing's heading our way and we're all in a big panic. Crazy.'

Bernard nodded his head before dragging his large, hairy body closer to the computer screen.

'Now there's this medical boffin who wants to give me some kind of revolutionary cancer treatment and I just don't know what to do. I can't fly back to England because our pilot's taken his ball home and even if I did make it, a bloody great blazing boulder's going to land in our back garden and incinerate me and the potting shed. The only consolation is that the vine-weevils will probably cop for it as well. What a huge stinking mess.'

Bernard's head again nodded. He then placed his head between his paws, snuffled and slowly blinked his rheumy eyes before reaching forward and licking the screen.

'Pack it in, you big soft bugger', chastened George half-heartedly. But how he secretly yearned for a cheekful of cascading, warm saliva.

'So, listen carefully Bernard and think carefully before you answer this next question because the fate of all civilisation rests on that monster brain of yours lurking between those ridiculously floppy ears.

'Are you ready?'

Bernard nodded his head.

'Is this asteroid thing going to crash into our planet? Right paw for yes, left paw for no. You know the script already.'

Bernard eased his head northward, rolled it about a bit then placed it back down again. He looked George in the eye, paused a tad and lifted his left paw.

'One more time.'

The dog again raised its left paw.

'Well that's quite a relief', said George. 'Bad news for you though Bernard.'

The dog lifted a querulous eye.

'Now the asteroid's not going to crash into us you'll have to sort those bloody vine-weevils out yourself.'

Behind the screen and the dog, Esme's dropping jaw was to be seen almost touching the surface of the best Axminster.

TWENTY-NINE

The Longworth family gathered in the parents' hotel bedroom for a house meeting.

George had decisions to make and he was being surprisingly, well, decisive.

He informed his wife and children that he was prepared to do another television interview with Sam and his mystery physician while he was also going along with this experimental treatment on offer. His reasoning was disarmingly simple. Firstly, he couldn't go home anyway, so now had the time, and secondly, what did he have to lose?

'And we're not going to die in an inferno from outer space, so I might as well,' he added, swishing a dismissive hand in the air.

'And how would you know that we're not going to die?' demanded Gaynor.

'Because Bernard says so. Ask Larry, he was with me when we spoke to him on that Sky Sports thing before.'

Larry shrugged his shoulders and said, 'Dad's right, Bernard reckons the asteroid's going to miss the planet so we're all going to be absolutely fine. NASA? What do they know? You can't get a better source than our Bernard.'

George cast his son a searching look to check he wasn't taking the piss. He narrowed his eyes, but just about gave him the benefit of the doubt.

'Have any of you lot wondered where we're going to stay now that the flight's been cancelled? asked Gaynor, deciding that she definitely needed to spend less time in the nursery. Her words were met with a thicket hedge of blank, clueless faces.

'No, I thought not,' she continued. 'Well the Longworth slave's sorted it. The hotel will let us stay, and for half the rate. They've had so many cancellations because of all this airline chaos and people aren't travelling anyway because of asteroid terror. I'm surprised they didn't turn around, tell us it's all our own fault and chuck us on to the streets.'

THIRTY

The White House administration – particularly the press office – was a steaming cauldron of pressure, worry and anxiety.

Despite an official sanction from head boy in the Oval office, the USA government's global warning about the official NASA tracking of a rogue asteroid had generated much criticism. Several world leaders and high-flying officials pointed to an over-reaction from the world's most powerful nation leading to the creation of unnecessary panic across many tiers of society. Incidents of civil unrest were at a containable level, but stock markets had tumbled, cash was being hoarded and ordinary citizens continued to buy unfeasibly large quantities of dried and tinned food, leading to empty shelves in the shops. Thousands of back gardens and cellars had been turned into makeshift shelters, houses had been fortified, guns stashed, while property demand in the more remote parts of every country had soared. Many transport systems were struggling to cope, but it was airline industry that was suffering the most serious disruption as the Longworths had discovered to their cost.

Laura Pitt, director of strategic communications in the White House press office was feeling the strain. Her original bulletin to the world – which she had deemed reasonably circumspect – was now regarded as too alarmist, yet colleagues on higher pay scales than hers were insisting that nations needed to be kept informed and it was Laura the wordsmith who was charged with the task of providing soothing solace about outer space.

Laura decided she needed help and asked her secretary to contact professor David Emmerson – the NASA expert – on the telephone. Ten minutes later and her request was granted. She was hoping the scientist would be able to calm some turbulent waters, but professor Emmerson wasn't forthcoming with too many reassuring noises.

Clarity, he explained, was hard to come by. The asteroid had skipped its customary orbit and was careering at a rate of knots in the general direction of the earth. Only when it was nearer would the scientists be able to make predictions with any further degree of certainty. His responsibility, he repeated, was to warn of a clear and threatening danger. He would not forecast that the Earth was about to be smashed to smithereens, equally, he could not reassure agog millions of his fellow human beings that life was set to cascade down its customary cheery path. His fence was erected, and he was obstinately sitting right on top of it.

'How long before you can be more certain?' asked Laura.

'At least another week. We're tracking the asteroid continually, but as yet it's still too far away for me to make any commitments.'

'What am I going to tell the President? What am I going to tell the entire population of a nervous planet?' wailed Laura.

'The truth?' ventured professor Emmerson. 'Always the best policy.'

'Not always in this job,' Laura mumbled under her breath before thanking the professor and wishing him a good day.

'I'll be in touch but be sure to let me know if anything changes.'

THIRTY-ONE

S am the man was eagerly looking forward to having George back on his show.

The affable Aboriginal knew that the ratings would again be sky high as his Pommie friend continued to make headlines all over the world without trying very hard at all. Indeed, without speaking to any journos at all either. Apart from his good self of course. And he had a great new angle on the story to deliver to an expectant home nation and beyond. The Hyena would be weeping into his keyboard when Sam introduced Dr Saul Sorensen to a hushed studio audience, the man destined to save George's life with his new miracle cure for stomach cancer. Sam briefly reflected that no medic had actually told George that he was dying, but what the hell, this was showbiz and who was it who had said, "never let the truth stand in the way of a good story."

He remembered...it was the Hyena, virtually every week. Who else?

The studio boys had again done a great job for Sam's latest show, iridescent, blown-up shots of George's family adorned the walls alongside large colour images of new local hero Dr. Sorensen. There was even a grainy satellite shot of the Longworth house back home in England. If George leaned forward and squinted hard enough, he could just about make out his greenhouse.

It had been agreed that just George and Dr. Sorensen would accompany Sam in the studio, despite Larry's protestations. Fifteen minutes of fame hadn't been enough for Longworth junior. Anyone lending any credence to his personal social media page would be led to believe that many years of multi-media magnificence lay in store for lamb chop Larry.

A few hours before the show, Sam sat with George and Dr. Sorensen and laid out an on-the-hoof plan of the various directions the programme would take...bit of background, asteroid up-date, family news, devastated about not being able to fly back home, the silver lining now attached etc, etc. Enter Dr. Sorensen waxing lyrical about his fabulous medical breakthrough, George's eternal gratitude, blah, blah.

'It is without doubt', Sam opined, with a sage nod of the head, 'one hell of a chat show bouncing along on the back of a great tale. Scripts? Who needs scripts? Scripts are for wimps.'

▼

The cameras rolled, and Sam soon realised that he really ought to have prepared a proper script.

Nerves jangled a tad as the opening title shots lured a national audience, not that they needed a lot of luring. Sam introduced the familiar face that was George, picked his way through some well-known background, again seizing the opportunity to pay tribute to Jamal, his friend and sporting hero whose sad death in the jaws of a crocodile had brought them all together. George's story was not without its poignancy too, Sam reminding audience and viewers that their English friend was fighting a killer of his own, a killer far removed from the one that had brought about Jamal's shocking demise.

But, Sam assured, help was at hand, all eyes stage left as Dr. Sorensen was introduced, the new guest strolling into the limelight and taking his place alongside his two studio colleagues. Sam explained that the post-graduate research oncologist was undertaking vital research into the treatment of stomach cancer and had some important news to impart. Sam handed his new guest the floor.

Dr. Sorensen said, 'I've been working on this project for a number of years now and I believe I'm on the verge of a breakthrough. The affected cells can be attacked, and the cancer eradicated by the introduction of a genetically modified virus and now I'm ready to trial this treatment on a human volunteer.'

Sam looked across at George, waved a hand across the studio floor and added, 'And George is that volunteer human... assuming we're not all wiped out by this bad-ass asteroid dude before he gets the chance to try his miracle cure,' he added as a vaguely light-hearted aside.

'Well, that's not going to happen is it?' interjected George. 'The asteroid's not going to crash into Earth. No way. We can all sleep safely in our beds on that one…let me assure you of that.'

Sam and Dr. Sorensen both stared at George in amazement. The studio audience emitted a low collective murmur. Sam's wish that he'd knocked together a cogent script – a running order or even a list of half-prepared questions – intensified.

'Erm, how would you know that then George?' he asked, stepping warily into uncharted territory.

'Bernard told me.'

'Who's Bernard?'

'My dog.'

The audience emitted an audible gasp followed by a telling background hum. Sam looked at George, not sure whether to take him seriously or not. There was a smidgeon of significant dead air time as Sam struggled to piece together his next question.

'So…what kind of dog is Bernard then? A pointer? Does he point to the heavens with his doggy paw and read the stars?'

Sam's attempt to introduce a touch of levity impressed neither George nor the audience who barely raised a titter.

'No, he's not a bloody pointer,' replied George, rather testily. 'Bernard is a St Bernard, the most intelligent of dogs. He knows everything.'

'Including the course of a large asteroid hurtling through space?'

'Yes.'

Sam was now wondering how off course his own show was heading after George had chucked this wholly unexpected and outlandish forty-yard ball at him. He was aware that Dr. Sorensen badly wanted to further promote his appeal for cancer research funding but suspected that the watching nation was far more interested in George's stargazing mutt. He was right.

'So, Bernard's here in Australia with you then?'

'No, he's back home in England staying with my neighbour. I talk him on a computer using that Skype thing. I asked him about the asteroid and it's definitely going to miss Earth. He told me, and I trust him implicitly.'

'So, you've got a talking dog then?' asked Sam and immediately regretted his flippancy.

'No, of course not,' replied George, snapping slightly. 'But he understands me and has a way of communicating with me using a kind of sign language. Bernard's a genius in many ways.'

Sam thought for a few seconds before making a quick, head-strong decision.

'Okay George. Do you think we could we speak to Bernard, on Skype, here live in the studio, in a one-off special, perhaps in a couple of nights' time?'

This was Sam seizing the moment big style. Dr. Sorensen would have to wait for his free funding plug.

'I'll have to ask him first, but I don't think it will be a problem,' replied George.

The audience burst into enthusiastic, spontaneous applause and cheered raucously.

THIRTY-TWO

Gaynor was sitting on the edge of the hotel bed watching her husband live on television, her head sinking slowly into her hands.

The Great Griping One – the man who had so wearied of the many media hacks ferreting about in his private life – had wantonly and openly courted a whole new wallop of "unwanted" publicity. He was appearing on television again and, in her humble opinion, had virtually invited himself straight into the grasping claws of the Hyena and back on to the pages of the Sydney Bugle.

Gaynor, as ever, was on the money.

The Hyena was indeed lurking in his lair, watching the TV at his newsroom desk, initially jealous and leering at George as he appeared live on television. But as the interview moved on and took a new and wholly unexpected turn of direction, the Hyena started to drool, quickly believing there was a God. As George gushed forth about his amazing dog and its knowledge of celestial bodies – Bernard would definitely become a talking dog by the time rabid newspaper hacks had mangled and twisted the story – the Hyena grinned horribly, grabbed a pen and pad and scribbled a front-page headline of his own making.

Vigorously underlining his demand for a bold 72-point font, his front-page headline would read: "Has Asteroid-Cancer Man Lost His Marbles?"

The sub-heading was a twin-tier affair. It read: "Bonkers Pommie claims he has a genius talking dog."

This was followed by: "Bernard the St Bernard smarter than NASA scientists."

He briefly considered adding: "Phew, what a loony!" but a modicum of self-restraint won the day.

Let those bloody sub-editors argue with that lot, he told himself, slipping into smug mode, barking orders to the night editor across the editorial floor and typing furiously.

▼

George joined Gaynor and their kids in the parental hotel room and sensed he was in big bother.

Gaynor gushed, 'I can't believe you went on television to talk about a cure for your cancer and instead prattled on about Bernard like he was Patrick Moore reincarnate. You surely must have realised what an eccentric all this makes you look George, and as for talking to Bernard live on national television…George, I despair, I really do.'

'Social media sites are absolutely alive with the story Dad,' chirped in Larry, gawking constantly at his phone.

'I'll spare you most of the gruesome detail, but it's everywhere. Dog lovers all over the world are right behind you though. Others are less impressed. Can I please, please, go on the show with you Dad?' Larry was still determined to turn his fifteen minutes of fame into thirty. Preferably hours.

'I think we ought to leave our poor Dad alone,' said Katie, shuffling along to sit next to George at the bottom of the bed and placing an arm around his shoulders. 'Live television can have strange effects on people.'

'Well, you're not wrong there', groused Gaynor. 'One roll of the camera and George turns into a gibbering wreck who tells the world that his dog is some kind of super-talented space scientist. God only knows what that Reynolds journalist is going to make of it all.'

George looked sheepishly at his family and spoke quietly. 'Perhaps I was a bit rash,' he half mumbled. 'But he's a smart cookie is our Bernard. I have total confidence in him.'

Gaynor's head went back into her hands.

▼

Sam the Man also had some explaining to do, hand-wringing schedule planners, programme producers and even station owners forming a less than orderly queue to speak to their headstrong, maverick presenter. They too were somewhat taken aback by Sam's impromptu and totally unexpected invitation to talk to a nodding dog via a live video stream winging in from the other side of the world.

Sam merely exuded confidence and beaming smiles. 'Great telly though guys, isn't it?' was his shoulder-shrugging response to all concerns, accompanied by a series of huge guffaws.

Senior management looked at each other and struggled to find words of reply. This was because they struggled to disagree.

▼

George gave his neighbour Harry a ring to arrange the Skype chat with Bernard. He would talk to Bernard about it later.

Harry couldn't quite believe what he was hearing.

'Let me get this right. You're telling me that you're really going to talk to Bernard via on of these infernal computer video links live on Australian television.'

'Yep.'

'What are you going to talk about?'

'This asteroid thing. Bernard knows for certain that it's not going to collide with earth. He's told me already. Now he's going to tell me again, but this time live on television.'

Harry paused and wished he had a whisky.

'George. We've known each other for bloody years and we've always been straight with each other…so let me tell it as it is.'

'Okay.'

'Aren't you at risk of making a bit of prat out of yourself with this one?'

'Look Harry,' sighed George, 'I do know that. I also know that I've not got long here on Mother Earth what with this cancer bastard chomping away at me. All this bizarre stuff that's kicked off since I came to Australia has been the most amazing episode of my life, unusual, different, possibly even life-changing. I don't really know if fame is a good or a bad thing yet, but I do know that I'm giving it a try because even if I do end up as a prize prat, at least I'll only have a couple of years to live with it. If that.'

It was Harry's turn to sigh. 'You're right George. To hell and set fire to it. What time does our Esme have to get out of bed to sort this Skype thing?'

▼

Sam would interview just George and Dr. Sorensen during the one-off television special. Larry sulked even as he slept.

The medic had only been invited back on the show because he'd moaned about the raw deal doled out first time around, particularly his need to talk about funding. Sam had nodded sagely and agreed. There would still be lots of George and the rather spiffing story about the shaggy dog that could read the stars.

The show may even prove to be more eventful than people were anticipating because Sam the Man and Dr. Sorensen had indulged in a touch of knavery as they picked their way through the script. Sam, insistent on a script on this occasion, knew it was a bit of a risk, but had prepared a rather special – and unexpected – question to put to his Pommie friend, a real teaser going out live to an agog nation perched on the edge of its collective sofa.

▼

Professor David Emmerson – the NASA expert – picked up the telephone to Laura Pitt in the White House.

She was anxious for an up-date, anxious to appease a fretful President who wanted asteroid news. But the leader of the free world wanted good asteroid news only because he was only too aware that a fretful planet was in need of solace and comfort.

However, the professor wasn't delivering.

The asteroid – and it was a hefty beast he pointed out – was still hurtling towards Earth and it would come close. Well, close in meteorological terms anyway. He wasn't prepared to be any more precise. Not for a few more days anyway. No, he didn't care if the President was on Laura's back.

'Tell him about that daft dog in England, the one predicting the all-clear.'

Laura didn't know if Professor Emmerson was joking or not, but she thought she might give it a try.

THIRTY-THREE

George embarked on an early visit to the deserted floor of the live television studio and surveyed the scene.

The designers had done another fine job, new graphics and large striking photographs adorned the walls, including a library shot of a lugubrious St Bernard dog. Nowhere near as good-looking as the real thing though mused George.

On a large studio platform facing three comfortable-looking chairs in the middle of the interview floor was a thin, mid-size screen on which, George assumed, Bernard would appear via Skype. He'd better not have changed his mind about this bloody asteroid George thought to himself. Sam suddenly appeared, strolled across the wooden floor and shot George a disarmingly wide grin before joining him for a chat.

'Another night of great television looms then George' chirruped Sam, churning out his new mantra. 'The promotional boys have been plugging it mercilessly and they're predicting an audience of millions. We're going world-wide, there's even speculation that the President of the United States could be tuning in. I think this dog of yours is going to be more famous than me George. He's certainly smarter.'

George nodded. The enormity of what was to happen to him and his canine soul mate in less than a couple of hours was suddenly hitting home. He needed to distract himself and thought about whether Harry and Bernard had managed to sort out those pesky vine weevils in his glasshouse.

▼

Two hours later and the cameras rolled to broadcast the next instalment of the amazing adventures of an ordinary Englishman and his nuclear family as a more restrained Australian news magazine had recently described them.

Sam rattled through the background story for the benefit of anyone who didn't already know it, which was no-one, before reminding audience and viewers of George's jaw-dropping revelation just a few days earlier, that his faithful hound was a space scientist who knew no peers. Sam was quick to point out that Bernard the St Bernard was not a talking dog despite the ridiculous claims being put forward by a certain low-brow city newspaper, who were not only delivering second hand news, but had also got it spectacularly wrong. The scorn on Sam's face was writ large.

He then turned to Dr. Sorensen, delivered a little more background before allowing his guest to expand on the daring medical trial which, he confidently predicted, would save George's life. The researcher was then handed free rein to make his appeal for further funding, the real reason he was there. A happy physician handed the floor back to Sam and George, the man of the moment. The scene was set. The pre-arranged time had arrived. They were contacting England via Skype. It was late morning in Harry's house and it was Esme who answered the call.

George issued a friendly greeting to his neighbour, politely enquired as to how they all were and then asked for Bernard. The dog, slightly man-handled by the collar by a gasping Esme appeared on the studio screen and thumped his tail excitedly on the sofa when he saw his master's face on the laptop in front of him.

'Now then Bernard my boy. How the hell are you?' asked George.

The dog panted and reached forward to lick the screen with a big, drooling pink tongue. The studio audience howled with laughter.

Sam interjected, restored gravitas, and explained how, only a few days ago, Bernard had predicted that the asteroid heading towards Earth would not collide with the planet. This, the dog had achieved by responding with sign language when quizzed by his master George. The way it worked would soon become apparent.

Sam turned to George and gestured that the floor was all his. George nodded and turned to his dog on the screen. He spoke slowly and deliberately.

'Now Bernard, I realise that I've asked you this question before but I'm going to ask you again because there's a big wide world out there who wants to hear your opinion. So, you already know the script. After the question, lift your right paw for yes, left paw for no. Are you ready?'

Bernard lifted his right paw. The audience murmured.

'Is this asteroid thing going to crash into our planet?'

Bernard rolled his eyes, re-focused and looked at George. His tongue drooped from his mouth and he shook his head. Spots of saliva were sent splashing.

He then lifted his left paw.

The audience hummed.

George added, 'Are you absolutely sure Bernard?'

The dog raised its right paw.

The audience gasped and burst into noisy applause. There was much cheering in the back seats.

Sam beamed to the camera and an entranced nation before calling for calm and quiet. Having secured obedient attention, in a hushed, conspiratorial tone, he then said, 'And now I have a special announcement to make. George doesn't know what's going to happen next, neither does he know what I'm going to ask him to do next. But Dr. Sorensen is here with us and as you know this esteemed medic is going to try and save George's life with his revolutionary cancer treatment.

'I want Bernard to meet Dr. Sorensen.'

The researcher moved a few feet to be beside George and so appeared on the screen next to his would-be patient. Dr. Sorensen raised a hand of acknowledgement to Bernard and rather sheepishly said, 'Hello Bernard.' The dog swished its tail across Esme's sofa.

George looked across at Sam, but Sam was glancing anxiously up at the producer in the control box who had not been privy to Sam and Dr. Sorensen's knavish subterfuge. The producer was animated, either ecstatic with glee and heady expectation or having a heart attack. Sam wasn't sure which. At least there was a doctor in the house if it was the latter.

Sam quickly composed himself and looked across at George who was frowning, but in control.

'George,' said Sam. 'Dr. Sorensen is going to try and cure your cancer and we're going to try and find out if his treatment's going to work. We're going to do this by asking Bernard what he thinks about your chances here live on television, right here, right now. What do you say George? Is Bernard up for it?' Are you up for it?'

A hush fell over the audience and a heavy sense of expectation descended. George felt somewhat taken aback by Sam's unauthorised detour into uncharted territory. But he couldn't help liking the chap and reminded himself of his own bravado when Harry had suggested that his flirtation with fame could be the making of a world-renowned prat.

George sucked in a big breath and spoke to Sam. 'Now that Bernard's actually met Dr. Sorensen, I think he will be in a position to make an informed judgment. He already knows that I have cancer – he's one of those dogs who can sniff out the disease you know – and we've discussed it many times in the past. So, if you let me explain this new development to him first, then we'll give it a go.'

Sam nodded and replied,' The floor's all yours George.'

The studio lights dimmed, silence again descended, and George looked straight at Bernard who looked straight back at his master.

'Hi Bernie boy, me again. I've got another question for you. Another important one, so pay attention and don't doze off on me.'

Bernard blinked and looked serious.

'This guy next to me here is Dr. Sorensen, a research doctor and he's developed a revolutionary new cure for stomach cancer. But he needed a trial patient, so he's chosen me and I'm going ahead with the treatment. Are you with me so far?'

Bernard raised his right paw.

The audience gasped.

'Okay, so when he treats me, the question for you is… will it work? Am I going to survive this cancer? Am I going to live…for a bit longer, anyway? No guesswork on this one Bernie and I want the truth no matter what it is. No messing.'

Bernard flopped his head on to his paws and rolled his rheumy eyes. He looked sad. No paw was lifted. George looked at his faithful friend and waited a bit longer. The dog's eyes drooped to half-mast seemingly of their own accord. Bernard then nuzzled his head even deeper into his paws and fully closed his eyes. George nodded slowly. He knew the answer…he wasn't going to get one.

'Bernard doesn't know. He isn't sure. He doesn't want to get it wrong. I'll ask him another question instead.'

'By the way Bernard, listen to this one. Have you and handbag Harry sorted out those pesky vine weevils in my greenhouse yet?'

Bernard opened his eyes and raised his left paw.

'No?!' barked George. 'Bloody well get on with it then!'

The stunned studio audience broke into a welcome guffaw and gossiped excitedly amongst themselves.

THIRTY-FOUR

T here was a full squad family and friends turn-out for George's visit to Dr. Sorensen at the university hospital.

The Longworths – adults and siblings – were joined by Dylan who had been personally invited by George "because he can speak the language." Gaynor had cast George a worried frown and wondered whether her husband needed his head examined as well. Sam had also trotted along with the entourage and had basically invited himself. Gaynor suspected the TV broadcaster in Sam was on the trail of the next chapter in the saga of George and his worldly travails and once again she was right. But he had turned up at the hotel with two large cars and drivers, so was forgiven.

Dr. Sorensen invited the close members of family into his consulting room and engaged them in small talk.

'I believe I'm about to treat a renowned celebrity', he said. 'A chap almost as famous as his dog'.

George raised an eyebrow.

Dr. Sorensen continued, 'You may well have heard already, but the word is that no less a leading light than the President of the United States himself has seen Sam's show. He's quite relaxed about Bernard's asteroid prediction and is happy to go along with the good news if only because it's helped to take so much tension out of the situation in so many parts of the world. I'm afraid the airlines are a long way from back to normal yet, but let's have it right, if it wasn't for all the travel chaos you would all be back home in England and George wouldn't be having this treatment.'

There was a collective nodding of heads before a young nurse walked into the room. He handed George a large sheaf of papers to fill in before explaining that he needed to join him in a nearby treatment room for blood tests. Dr. Sorensen nodded his approval, ushering George and the nurse through the door. He then returned to the seat behind his desk and addressed the remaining members of the family.

'If the blood tests are okay, then we can start the treatment later today. My research work has been focused on the treatment and prevention of stomach cancer, trials suggesting that the affected cells can be attacked and eradicated by a genetically modified virus. This only involves injections and not any invasive surgery which is good news. I believe George is already taking chemotherapy drugs. I need your permission to stop these because they could affect the trial. Then you need to sign to agree to the trial.'

Gaynor nodded and said,' How confident are you that this treatment will work?'

Dr. Sorensen smiled, 'Well, I know that our canine friend Bernard wasn't prepared to commit himself, but I've been encouraged by the trials I've carried out in the lab and I'm hopeful for a positive outcome. The world is watching, and we all need George to respond. Right, we just need to wait a couple of hours for the results of the blood tests and if they're okay then we can get down to work. George needs to stay here, but perhaps you three may care to step out for a spot of lunch and I'll see you all later this afternoon.'

Gaynor, Larry and Katie joined Dylan and Sam in the waiting room where the two Australians were hotly debating whether the national rugby league team were quite the force they used to be. Some brightly coloured reef fish wriggled languidly in a bubbly, blue aquarium.

'The doc will soon have your husband back on the old bungee jump Mrs L,' chirruped Dylan, thrusting a vast mane of matted hair back over his shoulders. Gaynor imagined a small wire-haired terrier leaping over the hippie's shoulder. Sam hoisted his six feet two-inch frame out of its seat. He expanded his chest to 42psi and started to jabber excitedly.

'Apparently the President of the USA has been watching the shows,' he enthused. 'He's a big fan of Bernie boy and we're all international superstars.'

'Actually, that's not quite true,' interrupted Larry, reluctantly dragging himself away from his 'phone where he was still watching clips of the family's first television appearance with lots of him in it.

'An aide told the President about the shows and he was happy to go along with them because they gave the answer to the asteroid threat that he wanted to hear.'

Gaynor nodded sagely and said, 'Yes. I could believe that of him.'

'Whatever,' gushed Sam with a dismissive wave of his hand. 'We're still big news all over the world and that's all that matters.'

'Perhaps,' sniffed Gaynor. 'Now what about that spot of lunch that doctor Sorensen recommended. We'll come back later this afternoon and see how George has gone on with his blood tests.'

Sam leapt back to his feet. 'Okay people, the tucker's on me, well, it's on the television company anyway. You guys are legitimate, claimable expenses, which will certainly make a change from the fictitious ones. Do you have any idea how much these rugby league players can drink?'

The Longworth clan and assorted members of the back-up crew weaved their way through a labyrinth of seemingly interminable hospital corridors before emerging into bright early afternoon sunshine cascading warming rays on to the hospital's front garden. A chorus of black field crickets chirruped amid stems of swaying grasses. A green tree frog hopped across the lawn. On a none-too-distant highway, Holdens burbled and bustled.

A free-wheeling Sam the Man led the posse up the driveway where their cars awaited. So did the ambush. From behind the flaking trunk of a particularly imposing eucalyptus tree emerged the Hyena. A snapper slivered and skulked in his wake. The Hyena, digital recorder to the fore, tried to sidestep Sam in order to track down more interesting prey.

But Sam's rugby league pedigree failed him not. The former Queensland back row forward knocked together

235

some impressive footwork and grapple-tackled the hapless hack to the ground before hauling him to his feet and pushing him roughly up against the aforementioned eucalyptus. Sam growled and snarled in his face. 'Why don't you just leave us alone, you puny, half-baked phony parasite. These poor guys have suffered enough already without you keep leaping out of every nook and cranny and scaring them to death.'

Reynolds, shards of tree bark sticking painfully into his back, realised he was at the mercy of a fellow human who was by far his physical superior. But he sensed that no real damage was heading his way. He knew Sam couldn't afford the deluge of adverse publicity that would descend from a dizzy height if he decked a professional rival half his size in the grounds of a hospital. He responded with a feisty verbal challenge.

'George isn't suffering enough to stop him keep appearing on your bloody stupid television shows. All that stress before live television cameras can't be doing his heart or his blood pressure too many favours.'

'So that's it...you're still one spiteful, jealous guy Phil Reynolds,' snarled Sam. 'Watch it and weep.'

Sam reluctantly released his grip and stepped back from the tree, the Hyena slipping away, scowling and muttering darkly. The snapper followed him, turning and taking one last snatched shot before the pair scarpered.

Sam turned to the Longworths, shrugged his shoulders and said, 'Well that would have been the front page of the Bugle sorted – again – but there's one major flaw in the Hyena's latest paparazzi raid.'

'What's that?' asked Larry.

'No George caught in the lens.'

THIRTY-FIVE

George's blood tests were clear for the new treatment to begin.

Dr. Sorensen explained that the cancer-attacking virus would be introduced by injection into the patient's bloodstream. George could carry on his life much as normal – not that George's new life was anywhere near normal – and while his progress would be monitored at the hospital every few days, a visiting nurse would carry out the injections. With a little tutelage this task could eventually be handed over to members of the family. George imagined Larry approaching him whilst brandishing a dripping needle and turned ashen.

The family waited while George was administered with his first dose of medicine before Sam led all the posse back to the hotel where they settled on large sofas in the front reception. A picture of a rather cute short-eared rock-wallaby peered down on them. Larry was full of news from his American friend Michael Berlingo and his dad Maurice, the prophetic amateur astronomer with the amazing telescope in the attic.

'Michael tells me that his family is almost as famous as ours. The press and television guys over in the States have been swarming all over them ever since they predicted the arrival of this asteroid before all the boffins. They keep asking his dad whether it's going to collide with earth and wipe us all out. He doesn't really know, so guess what he's told them?'

'You're going to say that he also believes the world's cleverest dog's got it right aren't you?' replied Gaynor, a slightly wearisome tone entering her timbre. 'He and the President both. '

'One hundred per cent correct mother,' replied Larry.

'The world has gone mad. Quite, quite mad,' sighed Gaynor.

'Barking mad?' offered Sam who howled with laughter at his own joke, tears starting to flow down his chubby cheeks. Gaynor managed a weak smile and continued, 'Almost the entire population of planet earth is pinning all hopes of its survival and the survival of our future generations in the crazy belief that a daft dog and its even dafter owner know what they're talking about. This is all becoming a bit surreal for me. George can only be behaving in such an outlandish way because of this bloody cancer and because he thinks he's not got long to go…'

Gaynor's voice started to falter, and break and tears filled her eyes. Sam shifted along the sofa and placed his massive right arm around her quivering shoulders.

'We have to try and look on the bright side of life Mrs L,' he said, hugging her close to him. Gaynor winced slightly as she felt her collar bones compress. Sam continued, 'George would never have been given the chance to have this experimental treatment if it wasn't for all the publicity that's come his way, no matter how crazy it all seems. It's difficult to believe that we're even in debt to the Hyena, but that's the way it is. And let's face it, if the asteroid does miss and if Dr. Sorensen can cure him, then all this surreal stuff will have been worth it…won't it?'

Gaynor sniffed and snivelled but nodded her head in agreement. 'I know that I have to put my husband first and that I should feel grateful George has the chance to get well again. But as for all this media celebrity carry on… I just hate it. I can't believe that some people actually chase and covet this kind of stuff. I just want to go home back to my normal, humdrum existence protected by a welcome shield of anonymity. I miss my old life so much. I want to worry about George's vine weevils again. My God, I'm even missing my horrible year ten maths class and I never thought I'd hear myself say that. When are things going to be normal? When is there going to be a plane to fly me back to England?'

And then it was announced that NASA scientist, professor David Emmerson, was to make a live broadcast from the White House.

To America and to the world.

THIRTY-SIX

White House press guru Laura Pitt needed this dog out of her life.

The maintenance of standards under the aegis of a dithering, demagogue president was proving tiresomely difficult, so it was initially relief and happiness coursing through her veins when professor Emmerson rang to say that he was now prepared to go public with the latest scientific analysis of the celestial beast heading the way of Planet Earth. Laura quickly found herself skewered on the horns of a dilemma. On the one hand she realised that a serious asteroid strike could mean the death of millions and the breakdown of civilisation as she knew it. On the other hand, she didn't want that darn dog to be right. She had to dismiss such puerile thoughts and hope that professor Emmerson would bring some much-needed gravitas to the debate.

'I hope you're going to tell me that this asteroid's going to miss,' she said, teeth gritted.

Professor Emmerson drew a deep breath before replying, 'I can't be completely certain that it's not going to crash into us, but I am now prepared to put my name alongside some educated, well-researched predictions. Telescopes all over the world are trained on this object which is now nearer. Some mighty powerful computers are also on the case which means that we've been able to come up with some realistic projections. This is a big asteroid, bigger than a baseball stadium and it's hurtling towards us at about twenty-five kilometres a second. An impact, depending where on Earth it struck, could mean mass death and destruction...at the very least some serious implications for just about everybody on the planet.'

Professor Emmerson paused and drew in another deep breath. 'But we're forecasting a near miss. Best prediction is that the asteroid's going to pass us by about two hundred thousand miles away in less than a week's time.'

'Two hundred thousand miles'! exclaimed Laura. 'That's no near miss, that's a long way off, a very long way off. I don't understand what all the fuss has been about.'

'In terms of the utter vastness of space, that's a very near miss, believe you me. Our moon is further away from us than that and you can see the moon from your bedroom window most nights.'

'Okay', replied Laura, 'I bow to your superior knowledge on all things outer space. When's the televised broadcast?'

'Tomorrow night. Two of the president's top aides will be alongside me and basically we're there to spread reassurance and calm all these turbulent waters.'

It was Laura's turn to pause. 'Can I ask one thing of you professor?'

'Yes.'

'Don't mention the damn dog.'

THIRTY-SEVEN

Larry reluctantly dragged himself off his hotel bed and made his way to his parents' room.

His phone was in his hand. It may as well have been nailed to his hand. He entered. Dad was horizontal on the bed watching television.

Larry re-engaged with phone and, reading from the screen, informed his father that a top space scientist in America was to appear on national and international television tomorrow night to talk about the asteroid. Social media and more traditional, more reliable forms of media were confidently predicting that the professor would deliver the welcome message that the end of the world was not in fact nigh.

'I know,' replied George, without averting his eyes from the television set.

'What? So, you know all about this professor Emmerson guy? How?'

'No. I know that the world is safe from the asteroid. Bernard told us so…remember? Haven't you been paying attention to anything that's been going on? You need to get rid of that phone my lad and tune into the real world.'

Larry shook his head in dismay and decided that protest was futile. His mother walked into the room from the adjacent bathroom. Larry repeated the news he had told his father.

'Good,' she said. 'Perhaps then the airlines will stop messing about and we can all go home.'

'And what about my special treatment with Dr. Sorensen?' piped up George as he restlessly re-arranged the bed, piling up four pillows, two horizontal, two vertical, to create a most agreeable back-rest.

'What will happen to that if we all bugger off back to England?'

Gaynor's crestfallen face turned to Larry for inspiration in search of a meaningful answer, but Larry just bit his bottom lip and looked fierce.

'I think we all need to talk about this,' Gaynor said. 'I'm calling an emergency house meeting.'

▼

The house meeting was to take place later that evening in the Fat Badger steak and ale house down by the harbour. Gaynor had impudently asked George if he was available to socialise with his nearest and dearest or would another impromptu television appearance stand in the way? George had snorted in derision and indulged in a small sulk.

But all was sweetness and light in the restaurant/bar as George ordered drink and food from the hovering waiter. He was called Corey and bore more than a passing resemblance to a young Pat Cash.

Gaynor raised a toast to her family and then sipped her glass of chilled white wine, daughter Katie of the same persuasion. Larry greedily guzzled his lager before sending a picture of his half-empty schooner to his famous friend in America.

Gaynor then addressed her family: 'I suspect we're coming to the end of what can only be described as a memorable holiday. Memorable in as much as none of us can possibly ever forget the unbelievable events of the last few weeks. Some families remember holidays in this part of the world for surfing the crashing waves, barbecues on the beach, sun tans and the odd encounter with a strange-looking marsupial or two.

But not the bloody Longworths. Oh no. We have to be content with witnessing a national sporting hero being eaten by a crocodile, surreal television appearances about an asteroid that's going to destroy the earth, our photographs and made-up stories appearing in virtually every national newspaper, a dog that's famous in the White House and now George as the focal point of a revolutionary new cancer treatment. You really couldn't make it up. But now we're about to be told that the asteroid's going to miss our planet which means we can all go home and get on with our ordinary, really boring existences. Isn't that right George?'

'What?' said George, fiddling with his beer mat and staring through the window at the glistening sea beyond. He thought he saw a dorsal fin break the surface of the water but could not be sure. Beyond the breakwater, small sailing boats bobbed and curtsied.

Gaynor sighed and regained composure before speaking again, 'I said that it now seems the asteroid's going to miss us, so when it does, then we can all go home. Bernard was right all along.'

'He sure was. I was always confident,' piped up George.

Gaynor paused, took a slug of wine rather than a sip and continued. 'But we have a problem. A big problem, one that doesn't seem to have occurred to anyone else, except me, as usual.'

More blank faces and another uneasy silence.

'George's treatment takes at least a month and during that time he has to go back to the hospital for check-ups, progress reports, blood tests, the whole nine yards. He can't do that if he's waging a war against pesky vine weevils in his potting shed fifteen thousand miles away. I want to go home. I think we all want to go home really. I'm supposed to be back at school – as indeed is Larry – Katie's due back at work, yet here we all are, living in limbo land with a whole host of decisions to be made and George is sitting here staring out of the window and not listening – again.'

'What?' said George, whose attention had returned to cetacean-spotting. He pointed towards the water. 'Do you think that's a porpoise swimming in the harbour?'

▼

Two days later and professor David Emmerson told a waiting world what they wanted to hear.

In conjunction with the Minor Planet Center in Boston, Massachusetts – an institute wholly dedicated to the tracking of asteroids – he confidently forecast that the rogue asteroid – AJK 698768 – would pass close to the earth in the next 24 hours.

Pass close, but not collide. The safety margin meant that the worry was over.

He had wanted to say that there was still a smidgeon of uncertainty but introducing doubt had been ruled out by much higher authorities at the White House who wanted no more panic and alarm. There were stock markets to consider.

George and his family watched the television broadcast from the hotel bedroom. 'They might have given Bernard a bit of credit,' groused George sniffle as he reached for the remote control and stabbed the off button. 'He was the first to know we were all safe and now has been erased from history.'

'Back in the real world', said Gaynor, 'we now have to decide what we're going to do. Flights should be getting back to normal soon and living in a hotel room is starting to wear me down. So, family, speak to me, please.'

There was a knock on the door. It opened. Sam the Man walked in. The timing was perfect, uncanny even, and Gaynor regarded him with a suspicious eye. Their self-appointed sage, mentor and tour guide possessed an innate ability to be in the right place at the right time, usually with the right answers. But as much as Gaynor liked Sam for the stout chap he was and appreciated what he had done for them, the nagging notion that Sam was motivated by no small amount of self-interest – i.e. his flourishing broadcasting career – was a constant niggle.

Here they were with yet more big decisions to make and problems to unravel and here was Sam, probably armed with most of the solutions.

Gaynor explained to him their manifold dilemmas and how she at least would like to go home, not least because there were classrooms full of pupils demanding her attention. But now there was George and his newly-found fame, Katie and her newly-found boyfriend and Larry, who, despite his newly-found maturity, still thought it was great to be bunking off school…an unholy mess in almost every regard.

'George!' she half barked across the room at her husband. 'What do you want to do? Speak to me man. We need to make decisions, move on, we have to be more assertive.'

'Okay, you're right,' replied George. 'Assertive, er, right, yeh. I'll have a word with Bernard. See what he thinks. Larry, spark up that Sky Sports gadget.'

Gaynor's eyes reached for the heavens, but once again she held her tongue. If it hadn't been for George's condition it would have been unleashed at full chat.

Sam stayed with the family while Larry and his dad repaired to another room where George was to speak to Bernard on Skype. He asked to talk to his dog on his own and his wish had been granted. Ten minutes late and he was back.

'Bernard seems to think that it would be for the best if I completed the drug trial even if he's still not sure if it will work. I miss him so much though and I know that he misses me.'

'Yes, but is that what you want George?' demanded Gaynor. 'Do you really want to stop over here on your own?'

'I'll stop with him,' said Katie.

'So will I,' added Larry, with gusto.

'You two can't stay!' exclaimed Gaynor, her voice raised, but strained and breaking. 'We've all got responsibilities back home, school, work, more school, bills to pay…'

'Isn't our Dad a responsibility too?' whispered Katie, tears welling in her eyes. 'What's more important…a few weeks putting blonde streaks in teenagers' hair or Dad's recovery from cancer?'

Larry nodded in solemn agreement. He wished he'd thought of that.

A wave of remorse swept over Gaynor. The strain of the tumultuous events, which had so overwhelmed her family since they arrived in Australia, now broke the surface of swirling waters. It erupted like an undersea volcano. She burst into tears and flung herself on the bed.

Sam, who has held his silence during the family debate, wrested control. 'If you want my opinion – for what it's worth – then I have to agree with Katie. Surely George has to complete his treatment, even if it's only to find out if it's worked.'

Gaynor sat up again, drew a deep breath to compose herself and re-stated the reasons they needed to go back to England.

But she sensed she was on the back foot from the outset. The more reasons she gave, the more her sympathy for George increased, and as her words petered out, she found herself thinking about ways they could make an extended stay work. She could surely convince school to let her have time off on compassionate grounds. Larry could do all his school work over the internet and was Katie's job as a half-interested hair washer really worth fretting about?

Then Sam spoke. 'I've taken the liberty of speaking to the big noises at the television studio about your dilemma and they've come up with a special deal. They've agreed to pay for all your accommodation, fund a daily tucker allowance with a few tinnies thrown in and they're going to make a substantial donation toward Dr. Sorensen's research work. Quite generous really.'

'Would the price we pay be more television appearances?' 'asked Gaynor, pointedly.

'Well, perhaps just one,' half-whispered Sam, his tone humble, almost apologetic. 'We've already put out the donation story on the news bulletins and we'd like to run a few lines about how George is doing and feeling during his new revolutionary treatment. And I thought we would invite young Larry to appear alongside him live in the studios... you know, dad and son, man and boy, solid crew together at the heart of a fate-torn family, Poms under the pump... that kind of thing.'

Larry put down his phone for the first time ever and jumped up and down in excitement.

'Oh yeh!' he exclaimed. 'This has just got to happen!'

Gaynor's eyes strayed across the room and focused on a beaming Sam.

She struggled to work out which of two competing emotions was winning the battle for her baffled head... disdainful disapproval or deep admiration.

But she knew one thing for certain.

The decision was made.

THIRTY-EIGHT

The asteroid missed the earth by 244,000miles. A near miss.

George spoke to Bernard on Skype to congratulate his perceptive pet on the accuracy of his forecast, while professor Emmerson rang Laura Pitt in the White House to indulge in a tiny gloat regarding the accuracy of his predictions. In Washington, Bernard's name was mentioned in the Upper House of Congress, while back in Australia, a Facebook campaign was set up calling for Bernard to be flown Down Under so he could replace the current Prime Minister in Canberra.

And George was back live on Australian television. With Larry. Dad in the limelight, son trying to steal it. The script according to Sam was one of compassion and camaraderie between father and son in the face of adversity. Sam would have his audience weeping into their cold ones. But Larry was keen to cover himself and his American friend in glory and the more Sam listened to his story the more he realised the vital role Longworth junior had played in the heady experiences of the last few weeks.

And when Larry exclusively revealed that it was his earlier internet contact with his American friend Michael Berlingo and his star-gazing dad which had unearthed initial evidence of the rogue asteroid, then Sam had to admit that he was rather impressed. He also reflected that if it hadn't been for Larry's dogged pursuit of the rock from outer space, then soul buddy Jamal Jawai would almost certainly be alive today. Sam had to dismiss such thoughts from his mind. Larry didn't decide fate, just went along with it.

When Sam did manage to divert attention back to George, his guest revealed that he was going to stay in Australia and continue with his cancer treatment with all his family by his side. A nation was heartened. George thanked the television station for their support and generous financial backing, Sam adding that the studio had received hundreds of messages and cards for George from well-wishers all over the country – even though he was a Pom.

George had smiled weakly and told his audience that his regular visits to Dr. Sorensen had been encouraging. Side-effects, he had been warned, included and food and drink tasting strange. He informed his audience that his last few schooners of lager had reminded him of antiseptic mouthwash but felt sure this was nothing to do with the cancer…it was just how Australian lager always tasted.

George cast Sam a smug grin as a tacit message flitted across the studio floor – best not to take on a veteran Pom well-seasoned on the piss-taking front.

▼

Dr. Sorensen ushered George into his consulting room with a kindly smile and a beckoning flourish of his hand.

He enquired as to his patient's general health and asked if his recent lager intake was still tasting like something you should brush your teeth with. George grinned and nodded. Dr. Sorensen had clearly watched his latest television appearance and had got the joke…unlike many of his fellow Australians looking in.

The doctor slipped into stern, professional mode and asked George if he really was experiencing any genuine side-effects following the start of his new treatment. George confessed to feeling tired, not having a great appetite and missing home, well, missing Bernard really. But these were symptoms readily associated with the previous chemotherapy drugs, so all in all, he remained reasonably chipper.

Dr. Sorensen chewed the end of his pen pensively and said, 'If the truth be known, we're in uncharted territory when it comes to side-effects, simply because the treatment is so new. You're our first human trialist, which is why your contributions will be invaluable. So, you're generally feeling pretty good then?'

George nodded. 'I was sick all over the floor in a bar the other week but that's not happened since.'

'Mm…but that was probably our terrible Australian lager again though wasn't it?'

George chuckled. The surgeon, doubtless handy with a scalpel, also had a cutting sense of humour George could readily identify with.

Dr. Sorensen told George that he needed to give another blood sample before he left that day, adding that the results of previous tests would be known in the next few days, results which should show if the new treatment was working.

'We're all with you all the way,' added Dr. Sorensen. 'Hospital staff, medics, nurses…an entire nation is with you in fact. If goodwill and best wishes were all you needed to recover, you'd be running the Sydney marathon next weekend.'

THIRTY-NINE

Gaynor picked up the trilling phone on the bedside table in her hotel room and recognised the gruff but friendly tones of Sam the Man on the other end of the line.

He informed her that he had some great news. The coming weekend was to witness a special commemorative rugby league game in memory of Jamal Jawai whose life and sporting career had been so tragically cut short. The game, between Jamal's old club, the Sydney Barracudas, and a select side consisting of the finest Aboriginal talent in the NRL, would also serve to commemorate Aboriginal Day, the start of a week-long celebration of the culture and achievements of Aboriginal and Torres Strait Islander peoples.

The full Longworth squad – along with Dylan – were invited as VIP guests of honour while Jenny, Jamal's life coach and sporting counsellor during his vulnerable, formative years was also to attend. She would sit alongside them in a special hospitality box in the iconic ANZ stadium in Sydney.

If George was feeling up to it, Sam added, he might consider an invitation to start the game in the front row. Gaynor chuckled at Sam's outlandish suggestion and beefed up the badinage.

'In light of his condition', she replied, 'he might be better on the wing. The hospital wing.'

Sam returned the chortle and returned to the real world.

'Seriously though, we would like him to go down to the pitch and kick off. Then he can scuttle back to the hospitality box and watch the Aboriginals splatter the Barracudas all over the paddock.'

'I'm sure that is something we can all enjoy,' retorted Gaynor uncertainly. 'Is the game being televised?'

'Being beamed all over Australia and beyond,' replied Sam, his tone imbued with a smidgeon of pride. 'It's just a pity Bernard isn't available for selection. He could play in the pack.'

▼

The day of the big game dawned bright and fair, and after breakfast, two rather swish, chauffeur-driven saloon cars pulled up outside the Longworths' hotel to pick up the passengers who would be pampered.

Sam was in the first car, in the front next to the driver and swivelled on his seat to speak to George, Gaynor and Larry in the rear. Jenny, Katie and Dylan were in the back of the other car, Jenny looking rather abashed as the two young love parakeets billed and cooed and stroked each other's hair.

Sam outlined the itinerary for the day. Lunch and a boatload of wine would be followed by a formal introduction to Aboriginal players past and present down on the pitch followed by displays of indigenous art, dancing and music. Jenny would then read a tribute to Jamal after which there would be two more speeches from top brass in the NRL followed by a minute's applause. Then George would kick off the game, leave the pitch to take up his grandstand seat and feast upon a tray of tea and stickies. A second boatload of wine was in the chiller on demand. Other alcohol was available.

The cavalcade of two left the hotel for the stadium, gaily-coloured pennants danced and fluttered along the side of the road as they approached the arena. The Longworth family and supporting cast were escorted to their hospitality lounge where they wined and dined like royals at a state banquet with their feet tucked under the top trestle.

Replete and slightly tipsy, the esteemed guests made their way to their seats in the stadium, Sam steering George away from family and friends and escorting him down many flights of concrete steps to pitch-side, then along the half-way line to the centre spot. The Aboriginal display troupes and dancers, their lithe bodies daubed with painted patterns and images, were making their way off the pitch as George and Sam made their way on.

George took a few seconds to look around him and drink in the atmosphere following the bottle of boisterous red wine he had quaffed with lunch.

The stadium was truly enormous. Rising tiers of seats were filled with cheering fans. Flags and banners bobbed and fluttered. Overhead, skeins of seabirds mewed and meandered. George felt rather overwhelmed by it all. Music blared, and fireworks soared into the air as the players and officials entered the arena and walked up to the centre spot. George gazed at an array of enormous thighs supporting enormous shoulders coming towards him and felt strangely insignificant. A hugely muscled Aboriginal player shook him warmly by the hand then slapped Sam across the shoulders. The heavily tattooed captain of the Barracudas also took George's hand and offered him warm greetings in a thick Australian accent.

The two team skippers briefly embraced and tossed a coin before both sides dispersed either side of the half-way line, the players carrying out rather outlandish warming-up exercises involving whirring arms and lifting knees. The huge crowd roared and bayed.

Sam took a ball from under his arm, placed it upright on the centre spot, turned and spoke.

'Right George. You're going to kick off, so you just boot the ball as far as you can towards the Aboriginal guys. Don't worry, it's not really the start of the game, just ceremonial. We'll re-start the match as soon as you're back in the hospitality sheds blowing the froth off a big one.'

George nodded, took a few unsteady steps backwards then paced purposefully towards the ball and unleashed his right foot. He struck it with as much force as he could muster and immediately felt dizzy. He looked around him, his focus blurred, then he looked upwards and the sky started to spin. He felt a stabbing, numbing pain in his chest. George looked across at Sam, cried 'help me' and collapsed backwards on to the turf in a heap, his head bouncing up off the bone-dry surface.

Sam, momentarily frozen in time, gazed in astonishment as George lay motionless on the grass. The pause was fleeting. Sam quickly ran over, bent over his friend and felt for a pulse on his wrist. He could not detect one. He waved his arms frantically in the air and as players from both sides dashed over, Sam gave George the kiss of life, breaking away sporadically to beat his chest furiously with his fists as mulled tears rolled down the big man's cheeks. On the touchline, the electric cart used to ferry injured players off the field raced over to the middle of the arena. Both team doctors were on board and jumped off on arrival, pushing roughly through the gathered throng of players and taking over from a near hysterical Sam. They gave George oxygen and tried to resuscitate him. They did not succeed.

Every man, woman and child in the stadium was hushed, out of their seats, standing in shock and awe. The silence was ghastly.

FORTY

Harry Pickford tossed and turned in his bed. Sleep had been difficult to come by all night and now at 6.00am matters hadn't changed much.

He rubbed his eyes, groused under his breath and climbed from under the duvet. He visited the bathroom and made his way down to the kitchen to boil the kettle. Bernard would be fast asleep in his basket in the corner by the washing machine. He would try not to wake him.

But Bernard was not in his basket. He was lying in the middle of the kitchen floor, his head rolled over to one side at a grotesque angle, his paws tucked unnaturally into his body, his eyes wide open, unmoving and unblinking. Harry knew straight away. He just knew.

He dashed frantically back up the stairs, shook his sleeping wife Esme and cried, 'It's Bernard…I've got to ring George…where's you mobile…what's his number?'

'What's wrong?'

'It's Bernard…he's…what's George's number?'

'Harry, you know damn well George hasn't got a mobile. Don't you remember?… 'infernal claptrap of a contraption.''

'Yes, sorry.'

'I've got Larry's number here in my contacts. Will he do? He's probably with his dad or at least nearby.'

'Okay.'

Esme rang Larry and he answered almost at once. He was crying.

'You've heard the news already then?' Larry wailed.

'News?'

'About Dad?'

'No, what about him?'

Larry, voice breaking and sobbing almost uncontrollably, described how his dad had collapsed on the pitch as he conducted a ceremonial opening at a rugby league stadium. Medics had rushed him to hospital and treated him on the way, but he had died before they got there. Sam had gone with him in the ambulance then rang a short time later to tell them he thought George had suffered a massive heart attack. The doctors tried valiantly but had failed to save him.

Esme burst into tears and told Larry she felt so sorry for them all, but she had to go. She would ring Gaynor later. Now was not the right time.

Esme ended the call, turned to Harry and said, 'George is dead. A heart-attack.'

Harry slumped down heavily on the side of the bed and placed his head in his hands.

'When?' he asked.

'Not too sure exactly. But within the last hour I would say. Isn't that just terrible.'

Harry was silent. His face was ashen. He looked stunned.

'Bernard's dead too', he whispered. 'I found him flat out on the kitchen floor when I got up.'

Harry looked at Esme and knew he would remember his next few words for the rest of his life.

'Bernard and George. Beloved dog and beloved master. They died at the same time.'

Part Three

"How lucky I am to have something
that makes saying goodbye so hard"

Winnie the Pooh

ONE

T he hotel receptionist had closed the curtains and placed a "do not disturb" sign on the door as Gaynor, her children, Jenny and Sam met in a small conference room near the lobby of the hotel.

It had been two days since George and Bernard had died. The news had hit headlines all over the world, particularly in Australia where much had been made of the freakish timing. It had been worked out that Bernard had died just a few minutes after his master. Dedicated dog lovers all over the world nodded sagely and declared they were not surprised.

During this time many tears were also spilled, and many hearts ached. But now the stark reality of the situation was starting to hit home for Gaynor and her reduced family. George had died 15,000 miles away from home and 15,000 miles away from his beloved dog and best friend. And somehow his family needed to get father and husband back to England.

Harry had called a vet to his home. She had confirmed his worst fears and told him that Bernard had probably passed away in the early hours of the morning from a sudden and unpredictable heart attack. She offered to take the dog away and place him in a pet morgue until it was decided what would happen next. Harry had smiled gratefully and thanked her. He had then waited a few hours before ringing Gaynor to tell her the news about Bernard and pass on his sincere condolences following the death of her husband and his friend and neighbour of twenty years. They talked about the timings of the two sad events on that fateful, gruesome day. They concluded that master and dog had died in the same short space of time and that this link, this bond, this surreal cerebral connection between human and canine could not be explained and probably never would be. Gaynor's anguish increased when she thought about how, in the past, she had cast doubt and derision on George's affinity with his big daft dog.

But the past could not be retrieved, could not be changed, and now Gaynor was presented with the task of facing up to the present and the future without her soul buddy and life partner. She realised there was so much to do, so much to organise. Death brought with it officialdom, paperwork and reels of red tape at a time in life when you could really do without more stuff to tax your aching brain.

'We all need to go home,' she said, addressing everyone and repeating a common refrain. 'We need to get George home and that in itself is going to present us with severe problems and more financial worries, as if we haven't got enough to fret about already.'

'Well, surely your insurance will cover the cost of flying George back to England…won't it?' Sam pointed out.

Gaynor was not a person to blush easily. Many years in front of many school rooms full of challenging, intimidating teenagers had made her mentally strong, but on this occasion her cheeks turned crimson.

'Er…we don't have any insurance,' she confessed, looking sheepish. She waited for a reaction in the room, but there was none forthcoming, so she continued to speak.

'When I searched for travel insurance before we left and told the truth about George having treatment for stomach cancer, most companies didn't want to know. The ones who would provide cover wanted an absolute fortune, so much that it meant we couldn't afford to make the trip. I knew how much the holiday meant to everyone – even George, even if he was reluctant to admit it – so I decided to take a big risk and not bother with insurance. It was a gamble that's backfired and now we're in a big horrible mess because I know it costs an awful lot of money to fly a body back home.'

Gaynor burst into tears and Katie rushed to her mother's side and placed her arms around her shoulders.

Sam clambered to his feet and said, 'Excuse me for a few moments' and walked out of the room. Sam was gone for about ten minutes. When he walked back in, he was pushing his mobile phone into his side pocket.

'I've spoken to the big cheeses at the television station about your problems and they've agreed to pay all the costs to repatriate George. We feel perhaps the pressures of those live television interviews somehow contributed to George's untimely death and in the circumstances, think it's the least we can do.'

He paused before adding, 'And if you don't mind, I'll fly back to the Old Dart with you. I'll be there to help and support you, organise the safe dispatch and collection of George's body and generally look after you guys after all you've been through.' Sam's voice tailed off and was hushed as he added... 'as long as you don't mind of course.'

Gaynor smiled through teary eyes. She couldn't help thinking that Sam would be sending back news bulletins of the family's return to England, painting a poignant canvas of the sorrowful funeral and the general air of melancholy surrounding the whole sad saga.

But she didn't have it in her to take him to task. She believed that Sam was a good man at heart whose personal anguish throughout this most disconsolate of times had been genuine and sincere and that he did have their best interests at the forefront of his mind.

Sam looked benignly at an array of relieved and grateful faces and carried on because his largesse wasn't over yet.

'In light of the collective sadness we've all endured, including two of us here today who witnessed the horrible death of Jamal on that river bank, the station will also pay for Jenny and Dylan to fly to England for the funeral as well – assuming they want to go of course.'

Jenny, Dylan and Katie looked at each other and then at Sam and they too smiled through teary eyes.

The only frown in the room was a small one atop Larry's freckled face. He nudged Katie in the ribs leaned over and whispered hoarsely, 'Where's this Old Dart place and what are we going there for?'

TWO

George's on-going treatment for cancer and the experimental nature of that treatment meant that a post-mortem examination was required.

The pathologist who issued the findings of the autopsy did not shock the world. He reported that the deceased had suffered a major cardiac arrest, one which led directly to his death and that no blame was to be apportioned. He had found evidence of cancer in the stomach, but this too was not connected to George's death. He was unable to say whether the cancer had been reduced by the new treatment being trialled when George had died. His findings were of little clinical value to Dr. Sorensen, not least because his patient had perished too early into the new course of medication.

Dr. Sorensen had written a heartfelt letter to the Longworth family thanking them for their various roles in his experimental work and offering his sincere condolences. He added that his pioneering medical work would undoubtedly continue because of the public interest generated during and after George's treatment.

The day after, the family received another letter. It was from Phil Reynolds, aka the Hyena, the hack who leapt out from behind inanimate objects to harass and hector his prey. The unscrupulous journo who also poured vast quantities of alcohol down the necks of unsuspecting victims in his ruthless quest to ferret out a new and outrageous angle on the hot news of the day. The man inhabiting the bottom sewer of the gutter press.

However, as the letter outlined, the Hyena was no more. The woeful disguise sunglasses, the surreptitious digital recorder, the skulking dingo masquerading as a snapper by his side were no more too, banished to that great press hall in the sky. Phil Reynolds had handed in his resignation at the newspaper and was a new man, a reformed character, a member of the human race again, one who wanted to make his peace with the Longworths and apologise for his actions, actions which he believed could have been partly responsible for George's sad and untimely death.

Gaynor showed the letter to Sam. 'I'd heard on the grapevine that he'd quit,' grunted Sam. 'Apparently he's also set up a crowd-funding campaign on social media to help pay for George's flight home and hundreds of dollars have already rolled in.'

'And how on earth did he know we needed it?'

'Perhaps he didn't, just guessed, or perhaps it was the last string he pulled while he was still a fully signed up member of the scumbag squad,' replied Sam rather ungraciously. 'I don't think he found out by getting Dylan drunk again though.'

Sam handed back the letter and thought for a moment. He considered how the television station was paying for George's special flight arrangements and the extra fares of Jenny and Dylan, all of whom would be brought together for George's funeral and his re-union with Bernard back in the Old Dart, albeit a re-union in death brought about by wretched circumstances.

He then wondered if this gathering really ought not to be too sad, more a kind of celebration of the bizarre events which had brought so many diverse characters together. The marking of a series of random happenings which had produced one hell of a yarn if the truth be known and if this was the case, then everyone who played a part in the modern-day odyssey should re-gather to indulge in roistering they would never remember. Surely George and Bernard would have approved.

Then, as his thoughts deepened and his creative mind whirred, he thought about someone else who had truly been involved right from the start, indeed two people without whom this whole story may never have been writ. The American kid and his star-gazing dad up in their Texan garret...Michael and Maurice Berlingo.

The money that the Hyena was raising could pay for two transatlantic airfares to England and boost the lager fund to help raise the spirits.

Sam turned to Gaynor and said, 'Gaynor, hun, I've got another idea to run up your flagpole...and Larry might want to listen in as well.'

THREE

S am strolled out of the television studios and signed
a few autographs. The arrival of the Longworths and
their entourage had certainly raised his public profile
and, while he now knew that the happy ending he so desired
had gone the way of the kitchen sink, Sam's sympathetic
handling of the story had won him many friends and
admirers.

As he approached a line of cars, the door of a white Ford
opened unexpectedly, and a most familiar face clambered
out on to the sidewalk. Phil Reynolds, aka the Hyena, stood
directly in Sam's path and raised both arms in surrender.

'I'm unarmed,' he said. 'No concealed digital recorder,
no hidden camera, I've not even got a pen or a press pass.'

'What do you want then?' asked Sam menacingly.

'To apologise and make my peace,' said Reynolds.
'George's death upset me more than you can ever imagine,

and I feel partly to blame. I put him under a lot of stress, tracking down that Dylan guy then writing all those stories about George's cancer and how I belittled him and his family. It was wrong, I realise that now and I want to try and make amends.'

Reynolds move close to Sam and the two men eyed each other warily.

Reynolds explained that he'd quit his job on the newspaper to lead a less cut-throat existence, before adding, 'Did Gaynor show you my letter?'

Sam nodded.

'I set up the crowd-funding appeal, so I could try and pay back a kind of debt I feel that I owe. Thousands of dollars have rolled in and continue to do so. The money is all for the family and hopefully might help get them through the tragedy that's been George's death. And his dog.'

Sam's mind was churning. Previously he had thought about how George's demise should be the catalyst for a re-union of all those involved in this epic adventure. And if he was being honest with himself, the Hyena had played a role that could not be overlooked. He may have employed some highly dubious tactics, but he'd been the first journo on the scene when Jamal had died, while his exploitation of Dylan had led to the revelation about George's cancer. Without the Hyena's journalistic malpractice, Sam would not have entranced his biggest television audience ever with the dog who could predict the future. He thought again about his plan to reunite the whole cast of the story behind George's death and decided he needed to be true to himself. The Hyena was an integral part of it and so had to be invited.

And perhaps he'd better not call him the Hyena anymore.

Sam stretched out a hand of friendship which Reynolds took and embraced. Sam then explained his plan to fly the whole shooting match out to England for the funeral, the roll call to include his own former rival on the killing fields of the Sydney media/mafia premiership. Reynolds beamed with delight and announced that he was on board and would pay his own fares and expenses. The two men shook hands again and agreed to consign former antagonisms to the dustbin of history.

Sam rifled through his pockets in search of his phone. He needed to start talking flagpoles and ideas with Gaynor again. He also needed to run past her the notion of just one cameraman and a sound engineer joining the funeral party on the great sojourn. Just a couple of small dudes melting into the background, no invasions of privacy, no stressful live interviews, no worries. And he needed to tell her about the reformed character formerly known as the Hyena joining the entourage. Sam was pushing his luck again. Best beseeching, humble mode required.

▼

Larry's answered his ringing phone to speak to Michael Berlingo, top mate on Skype and the son of the talented Texan asteroid-spotter.

The mood was sombre. Michael passed on his sincere condolences to his English friend and his family following the sad loss of his father and the dog before asking – out of customary politeness rather than genuine expectation – if there was anything he and his dad could do to help at such a sad time.

The answer the young American received rather took him by surprise.

Larry said there most surely was and issued the invitation for Michael and Maurice to fly over to England for his dad's funeral and a mass get-together, all expenses paid.

Larry then explained the course of events since his dad had died, the offer of the television station to pay for the repatriation of George and the air fares of Dylan, Jenny and some dago journo who used to be a bastard but wasn't any more. The idea was to re-unite all those sitting in the scary seats of their recent, rip-roaring rollercoaster ride to pay their heart-felt tributes to George and Bernard. Hence the guest list would include their American cousins, the two-man Berlingo combo, the head of which had spotted the asteroid in the first place and set so many wheels in motion.

But at the same time as the funeral – or possibly a few hours later – they would also celebrate a story riddled with tragedy yet infused with the tangy flavours of international politics and intergalactic melodrama, and of course, a dazzling dog. 'We're all going to be there,' Larry enthused. 'Sam the Man was so keen, he's invited himself.'

Michael whistled softly down the phone and hollered for his pop.

FOUR

Sam had also invited himself to organise the return of George's body back to England without causing his family any undue anguish or worry.

He sought the services of a professional repatriation company – the television company was picking up the tab after all – and paid extra for the coffin to be carried in the hold of their flight home.

George would then be as close to his family and friends as possible, an aircraft floor and a closely-fitted carpet away. Sam hoped Gaynor would approve. Unless pushed, he decided he would tell her after they had taken off, or even landed in England. He had once seen a documentary about the variety of cargo loaded on to larger passenger planes, other than suitcases. One flight had taken off with two tonnes of smoked salmon and a vintage MG sports car stashed just a few feet below the air stewards' soft shuffle.

Sam decided not to ask what else would be in the cargo hold on their particular flight.

Gaynor was happy, and more than a tad relieved to let Sam do all the organising, at least on the Australian side of the world. The big Aboriginal's warm personality and considerable physical presence – not to mention his recently enhanced celebrity status – combined to allow him to scythe effortlessly through thickets of red tape. He stormed through bureaucracy like he had stormed through the New South Wales front row during his hey-lads-hey days in an outstanding Queensland State of Origin side. Pen-pushing, paperwork-wavers were flicked effortlessly to one side like a pesky opposition scrum-half.

▼

The full complement of travellers met in the Longworths' hotel the evening before their morning flight to England. The Americans had been contacted again, were up for the big get-together and Sam had booked their flight tickets on-line. They would all meet up at the Longworth home back in the Old Dart.

Sam had organised champagne cocktails at the hotel bar. Jenny wore a new black dress especially bought for the occasion and Dylan had undergone a haircut. Well, Katie had trimmed it slightly while a nervous Prestige fussed and fretted. Larry had been ordered to leave his phone in his room and not to sulk, the promise of a full cocktail allowance just about winning him over.

The atmosphere was subdued, but convivial. Sam had told a sceptical Gaynor about his decision to invite the

Hyena back to England and Gaynor had not found the will within her to object. Live and let live. If only.

Inwardly though she had made a big decision. She would let Sam do the walk and talk while they were in Australia, but once back in England – on home turf – she would wrest back control. This was her family, her husband's funeral and she would be in charge. Her train of thought was interrupted when Sam nudged her knee, nodded towards the door and whispered, 'The Hyena, he's here.'

Gaynor whispered back, 'We can't call him that. What's his real name again?'

'Phil, Phil Reynolds.'

Sam rose to greet the last member of the expeditionary party and shook his hand. Gaynor passed a careful eye over the man who had played the role of personal predator for most of their alleged holiday. He was dressed soberly, in keeping with the nature of the occasion. Larry cast him a disparaging glance, of the opinion that hand-pressed slacks and a pretend Ben Sherman shirt were a complete disaster. But he maintained his silence and dispatched his third cocktail with indecent haste. One more and he would have the courage to sneak back up to his room and retrieve his phone.

FIVE

The Airbus 380 touched down gracefully on English soil. There was no mist, there was no haze. A smattering of seagulls bleated and blathered high above a hangar roof.

During the flight, Sam had told Gaynor of the special cargo in the hold and she had accepted the news with good grace. She thought of how fate had been so unkind to the man who was already six feet below her. Her husband had made it to the other side of the world on a flight he dreaded before flinging himself fearlessly off a terrifying bungee jump without the need to change Speedos. He had survived a menacing asteroid, appeared live on national television, created the most famous dog in the world and possibly cured himself of cancer. A fatal heart attack had been on no-one's radar.

But this was the hand that fate had dealt and now Gaynor had to play her busted flush on a card table inhabited by a most unlikely cast of colourful characters. There was only one certainty. Gaynor knew she had to honour and remember George in a fashion that he would have appreciated, and she already thought she knew what he would have wanted.

▼

The Longworth family home was the first port of call for the party of travellers after their long flight from Australia. The company behind George's transportation had organised to store his body in a casket at the airport until it was required to be released for the funeral.

Harry and Esme were waiting outside their neighbours' front door as two taxis arrived from the airport shortly after midday. Many introductions were made, and many tears shed in the lounge before Gaynor and Esme went into the kitchen to organise cups of teas and trays of sandwiches. In the corner of the room Bernard's half-chewed dog bed lay empty and forlorn, another poignant reminder of irreplaceable loss and bonds broken. The Berlingos were shortly due to arrive and their sandwiches were placed on a plate and covered with silver foil.

Gaynor and Esme carried the rest of the food and drink into the sitting room where they ate standing up, Jenny and Sam talking to Harry, Katie and Dylan talking to Phil Reynolds, Gaynor and Esme talking to each other, Larry talking to his phone. There was much to discuss.

After a few minutes, a car pulled up outside and its engine was cut. Gaynor moved over to the window, surreptitiously pulled a curtain slightly to one side and peered out. It was a taxi and in it were a man and a younger man. Out of the back seat climbed a good-looking teenager with olive-coloured skin about Larry's age. Michael Berlingo Gaynor told herself.

The passenger front door of the car was already open, the back of a person she presumed to be Michael's father leaning inside to pay the driver was all that Gaynor could see. Then he eased his body out of the vehicle, lifted his head and turned around. The late to middle-aged man still had the dark braids in his hair he had probably styled with pride and care since his youth. They now contained streaks of grey and were probably shorter than they used to be, but they were still unmistakable and striking. The dark skin of his craggy face was wrinkled, the skin of his cheeks creased, but his deep-set brown eyes radiated sagacity, warmth and humour. Maurice Berlingo looked like he could be Sam the Man's dad. Maurice Berlingo was an indigenous Aboriginal.

Gaynor suddenly realised she was staring at him with her mouth open. Why she should feel so surprised she didn't really know, but she had never expected this. It was no big deal…but she thought Larry might have mentioned it, especially with Sam the Man and Jenny sipping small sherries next to the sideboard six feet away.

She turned from the window, grabbed her son's hand and led him from the lounge.

'You never told me Michael's dad was an Aboriginal', she hissed in his ear once they'd made it through the door into the hall.

'Is he?'…'I didn't know,' protested Larry, innocence writ large on his young face.

'You didn't know!' exclaimed his mother.

'No, I didn't know', came the indignant response. 'I only ever spoke to Michael on Skype and he never mentioned it. His Dad was always up in the attic, away with the stars as it were.

Why…does it matter?'

'Er, well, no, not really I suppose, not at all,' dithered his mother. 'It's just that…oh forget it. Anyway, your American friends are here,' she added as she propelled her son along the hallway, opened the front door and issued the statutory warm welcomes.

Michael and his dad hugged Larry and Gaynor, more condolences and pleasantries exchanged before the new guests were ushered through into what was becoming a rather congested lounge. More introductions were made amid an almost tangible element of surprise in the room. This was because Sam and Jenny were both surprised to see another Aboriginal in the room.

Maurice Berlingo wasn't surprised. His son had briefed him about the indigenous Australian connections ever since he'd spotted the rogue asteroid from his Texan loft, intrigued that observations taken in outer space either by telescope or the naked eye could unite communities divided by so much earthly geography.

Then Maurice started to speak to Jenny and Sam and many more pieces started to fall into place. Jenny detailed the night under the stars at the sacred site when she had first noticed the anomaly in the heavens. She re-told the story of her meeting with Larry and Jamal Jawai by the river, the gruesome death of Jamal in the jaws of a crocodile and the subsequent media circus which had snowballed to encompass the Earth's close encounter with destruction, the dog that saved the world, George's battle with cancer and subsequent death.

Maurice Berlingo nodded sagely, adding sadly, 'My wife Margaret died from cancer five years ago. Michael was only eleven and we took up star-gazing together to try and forget what we had both lost.'

'You poor things,' said Jenny quietly and rested her hand gently on Maurice Berlingo's wrist.

Sam took up the narrative, describing how his television show had sensitively handled Jamal's death and showcased the subsequent follow-up stories about George, his dog Bernard and the hospital trial into a possible cure for stomach cancer. Phil Reynolds was invited over to describe how he had broken the story about George's illness. His exact methods were rather conveniently shoulder-charged into the long grass, but Sam had long since forgiven these trespasses.

And so a long day drew to a close. Harry and Esme were the first to leave in the early evening shortly followed by the other invited guests who travelled by taxi to spend the next few nights in a nearby hotel.

This left Gaynor and her two children in their own home without George and Bernard for the first time.

Their sense of loss had never felt greater.

SIX

Gaynor had promised herself that she would seize the initiative once she was back on home soil and the next day did just that.

She understood that George would have wanted in death what he wanted in life…to be beside his beloved Bernard. His wife, possibly just as beloved, would join them later.

Gaynor had undertaken her research on the internet and knew that it was feasible for dog and master to be buried or cremated together. George hadn't been a particularly religious person, but he had been a choirboy in his youth, and his children had been baptised. Gaynor needed a friendly, understanding and compassionate vicar and she already knew where to find one.

▼

The Rev. Simon Heath carried two lightly sugared cups of tea into the lounge of the vicarage where Gaynor was settled on the edge of the sofa. The vicar already knew who she was.

The story she started to relate wasn't unfamiliar either. A young man, tech-savvy, the vicar had keenly followed the exploits of his very own parishioners on the other side of the world, not the only observer to be intrigued by the surreal escapades cascading into the lives of the once lowly Longworths.

He nodded with sympathy and understanding as Gaynor related the quite surreal adventures which had befallen them. In turn, the Rev. Heath informed her that he was fully conversant with the series of remarkable events which had led to this very meeting.

He added, 'I was a great admirer of Jamal Jawai and even though I'm a bit of a Brisbane Broncos fan, I was shocked and saddened to learn about what happened to him next to that river. It must have been so upsetting for your young Larry to witness that. I know all about what happened to you and your family after that tragic incident…I think just about everybody does.

And I think I know what you're going to ask me.'

Gaynor replaced her tea cup on the casual table and asked the vicar to continue just with the look of encouragement on her face.

'I think you want George and Bernard to be together in death. In the same resting place.'

Gaynor looked sad, but managed a small smile of appreciation and asked, 'Would that be possible?'

The vicar placed his hands together as if in prayer and lifted his head. 'The guidelines concerning shared funerals and other unorthodox wishes have relaxed over the last few years. I don't think it will be a problem, but I do think that cremation will be the easier option in terms of saving you from bureaucratic hassle. Are you alright with that?'

Gaynor nodded, 'I think so. George wasn't a particularly religious person. He didn't go to church much, hardly ever in fact…are you alright with that?'

'I can offer you a completely secular service at the crematorium if you wish, or a simple ceremony with a couple of basic hymns and a few simple prayers. This kind of service means less of me preaching, providing more chances for family and friends to speak and pay a more personal kind of respect.'

'I think that would suit everybody just fine,' replied Gaynor. 'I can think of at least one of our guests who likes to wax lyrical in front of a live audience.'

'So, you want me to help you organise all this?' asked the vicar.

'Yes, I do. Thank you so much Simon. You've been most understanding.'

▼

The crematorium was a bright modern building fronted by manicured lawns. Neat borders were planted with standard roses and horizontal cotoneasters bearing clusters of bright red berries. Flowering cherry trees lined the drive up which the funeral cortège carefully manoeuvred. A tangle of sparrows fussed and fluttered amid the foliage.

Professional undertakers eased two coffins out of the back of the hearse. The smaller of the two was placed on top of the other, the male mourners, Sam, Larry, Dylan, Phil Reynolds, Maurice and Michael Berlingo providing the shoulder support needed to carefully carry the wooden boxes into the building. They were followed by a slow train of family, friends and neighbours. Salty tears trickled into dampening handkerchiefs. The coffins were placed side by side before a simple altar bedecked with flowers, many of them grown in George's greenhouse where neighbour Harry had been a busy little bee.

The gathered throng sang "Onward Christian Soldiers", the service's only nod to religion, before the Rev. Heath addressed them. He did not linger. He spoke of George's courage in great adversity, of his love for his wife and children, his devotion to family life and the belief that his dog could understand every word uttered into his big floppy ears. Sceptics should not scoff he warned. Beliefs came in many shapes and forms and who was to demean the human right to one's own credo? Indeed, wasn't it the case that all religions rested unsteadily on foundations of suspicious, shifting sands, leaving every belief vulnerable to scepticism?

And on that note of slightly controversial secularity, the Rev. Heath handed the floor to Katie.

Katie read a poem by John Betjeman from his 'A Few Late Chrysanthemums' collection, in memory of her father's horticultural pursuits. She would have liked to have narrated a Betjeman ditty dedicated to the persecution of all matters vine weevil but discovered that the wryly comedic bard had failed to stray into this particular territory. It was a pity her dad wasn't into steam trains.

Larry stepped into the pulpit and spoke of his deep respect and admiration for his father, especially his tussle with cancer later in his life. He related the story of the nerve-shredding bungee jump early in their Australian adventure and how his plucky dad had taken the plunge unlike his wimp son who had lost his nerve late in the piece. In the gathered congregation Dylan nodded in reflective memory and smiled ruefully.

And then Larry gave way to Sam the Man.

Sam was dressed immaculately in a dark grey suit. His hair shone. His beard was trim. His eyes were moist. He took a deep breath, raised his head, looked upwards and raised his right arm.

'Today we have a roof over our heads, obscuring the view of the heavens high above our mortal souls,' he proclaimed. 'But up there among the stars is where this remarkable story starts. The story of why we are all gathered here today. We are here to mourn the man, his many colourful characteristics, the personality we have all lost while we also offer our sympathies to his family and friends.'

Sam paused for dramatic effect.

'But perhaps there are reasons to celebrate as well. The asteroid we so fretted about missed Earth, saving our civilisation from a fate which can barely be imagined. As part of this process George, his family and their dog Bernard brought to us all this very real threat of disaster, yet ultimately, they delivered salvation, wonderment, belief and joy to so many.

'Nations all over the world shared a united grief when George – and indeed Bernard – were so cruelly taken away from us. If the value of a man's life is to be judged by the number of people who shed a tear upon learning of his death, then George's time on earth was priceless.'

Sam wiped tears from both his plump cheeks and stepped down.

Rev. Heath started to read more Betjeman. There was a mechanical whirring nose and both coffins were lowered into the inferno below.

ONE YEAR LATER

Small ripples on the surface of the unhurried river
riffled the delicate light seeping from the sickle moon.
The oxbow lake was sluggish and dark, yet
strangely inviting. A shingleback lizard took a tentative drink
from the gently lapping shallows. The lizard was guarded
and wary. This was crocodile country. Sam the Man was also
guarded and wary for the same reason. He was sitting on the
river beach just a few yards inshore from the very spot where
Jamal Jawai had lost his life in the grip of gruesome reptilian
jaws. Sam was not alone. He was amongst friends – family
almost – the legacy of the Longworth saga still alive and
very much in evidence on the sacred Aboriginal site where
so many of its origins could be sourced.

A large blanket had been laid out on the sand. Sam was
in the company of Gaynor, Katie, Larry, Dylan, Michael
Berlingo and Phil Reynolds. Jenny was sitting next to

Maurice Berlingo, holding his hand and had never been happier.

The affinity between the two had been apparent from the day fate had thrust them together in the Longworth family lounge where they had gathered before saying their last goodbyes to George. The vast expanses of sea and land dividing the two ranging continents of Australasia and the Americas had proved no obstacle to their growing affection. Jamal Jawai's former NRL club had provided generous financial stability for Jenny after the shock death of the player she had done so much to nurture and encourage. She had used some of that money to fly to the southern States where she had gazed at the mesmerising night sky through the telescope in the attic of Maurice Berlingo's Texan home. In turn, Maurice had flown to New South Wales to join Jenny on the sacred Aboriginal site where she had first discovered the rogue asteroid in the same distant heavens. They had also discovered they were both so happy and content in each other's company.

They had been married on the same ancient site in a traditional Aboriginal service earlier that afternoon. Herbal plants had been burned to produce a fragrant smoke which was then fanned over the couple to provide healing properties and fend off evil spirits. Bride and groom had cast a stone each into the river, a representation of unity as their future life together ebbed and flowed around them.

Dylan and Katie were also sitting hand in hand on the blanket. Their relationship had also survived the separation of wearisome time zones and outlandish geography. Gaynor watched her daughter giggle and chortle in the arms of the young man who was "good with ropes". She suspected that one day Dylan would tie the one knot that really mattered. She wondered if he would have his hair cut first.

Gaynor and Phil Reynolds had also kept in touch since the funeral in England. Gaynor suspected that the reformed journo – who now wrote features for a monthly gardening magazine – would have liked a deeper relationship with the English woman he had once pounced upon from behind inanimate objects. But she was still some distance from moving in that direction. She was even yet to tell him that they used to call him the Hyena.

Meanwhile, her memories of George remained strong and while they would surely fade with time, they would never die. Nor would she want them to.

Gaynor felt certain she would never need daily reminders of the man she had loved so much for nearly thirty years, but she had got one anyway.

It might have been hospitable to invite Harry and Esme to join them for the great re-union on the sacred riverside site Down Under.

But her neighbours had far more pressing duties to perform back home.

They had been charged with the task of looking after Bernard junior, the St Bernard puppy their neighbours had acquired six months earlier.

Now all Gaynor had to do was make sure the new dog in her life understood every word she uttered into his ridiculously floppy ears.